RETURN TO BALANDRA

Returning to her Caribbean island home, Suzanne looks forward to being with her parents again, but most of all she longs to see Wim van Branden, a coffee planter she has known all her life. There have been many changes during her absence and she senses an undercurrent of emotions she cannot understand. But her unhappy mother still strives to manipulate her family, even seeking to precipitate Suzanne's future without her knowledge.

DOM

Library at Home Service
Community Services
Hounslow Library, CentreSpace
24 Treaty Centre, High Street
Hounslow TW3 1ES

YOUR COMMUNITY
YOUR SERVICES

0	1	2	3	4	5	6	7	8	9
510	161	7912	943		3325	706		688	
240	7751			6414		846	349	628	
	9141		7653			316	600	2438 1588	
						6306		638	
							3087	3488	929
							3457	9578	
							7927		

P10-L-2061

Love is
a time of enchantment:
in it all days are fair and all fields
green. Youth is blest by it,
old age made benign: the eyes of love see
roses blooming in December,
and sunshine through rain. Verily
is the time of true-love
a time of enchantment—and
Oh! how eager is woman
to be bewitched!

GRACE DRIVER

RETURN TO BALANDRA

Complete and Unabridged

ULVERSCROFT
Leicester

First published in Great Britain in 1982 by
Robert Hale Ltd.,
London

First Large Print Edition
published November 1990
by arrangement with
Robert Hale Ltd.,
London

British Library CIP Data

Driver, Grace
 Return to Balandra.—Large print ed.—
 Ulverscroft large print series: romance
 I. Title
 823′.914

 ISBN 0-7089-2310-0

Published by
F. A. Thorpe (Publishing) Ltd.
Anstey, Leicestershire
Set by Rowland Phototypesetting Ltd.
Bury St. Edmunds, Suffolk
Printed and bound in Great Britain by
T. J. Press (Padstow) Ltd., Padstow, Cornwall

1

FROM her seat in the small aircraft Suzanne Grayson looked out along the silver wing and then down to the necklace of jade green islands below. Set in the sparkling blue Caribbean, they lay serene in the tropical sun, silver sands running out to sea beneath the crystal clear water.

Larger than the other nearby islands, and set amidst them like an oval medallion, she could see Balandra, its extinct volcano rising from the peak of its highest bluey-mauve mountain. And beyond the mountains, where the rain forest ended, the vast acres of Wim van Branden's coffee estate, which covered the slopes to the west and extended almost down to the outskirts of the capital, St. Louis.

Now she could see the landing-strip. It looked diminutive between the patches of lush green vegetation, and Suzanne felt a tight knot in her midriff as the pilot began the steep descent. She closed her eyes until she felt a slight bump and knew they were safely down, then with a sigh of relief, unfastened her safety belt.

Presently the door slid open, and together with the half-dozen other passengers, she collected her belongings and made her way to the exit.

In her blue silk jersey trouser-suit she made a slender silhouette against the glittering rays of the sun. Over her arm, her tawny fox coat, now so unnecessary, seemed to develop a life of its own as it repeatedly slipped and slithered from her grasp. She hauled it into submission, then let her eyes roam over the well-remembered scene.

The soft warm wind blew a strand of her long blonde hair across her eyes. She brushed it away with her free hand, then reached into her bulky shoulder-bag for her sunglasses. She put them on and looked towards the visitors' enclosure. She could see her mother, but pleased as she was to know that she was there, she searched in vain for the one person she longed to see after her three years away from home.

Suzanne waved enthusiastically, then followed the small group of passengers towards the improvised terminal building and gave her attention to the collection of her luggage and customs formalities.

When she finally emerged, she was struggling with two pieces of luggage and her coat. Her ungainly shoulder-bag was slung over one arm so that it slumped against her long, slim legs as she walked towards her mother to dump her cargo.

Helene Grayson, in a simple cream linen suit and tangerine silk blouse of unmistakable French origin, remained where she was. She watched her daughter approach with increasing surprise. Three years ago she had been a mere schoolgirl, and now she was transformed into an attractive young woman.

"Suzanne, *chérie!*"

They hugged one another, then Helene stood back, her large brown eyes now regarding Suzanne in a new light.

Suzanne self-consciously looked about her.

"Where's Papa?"

"He went to park the car." Helene turned. "Ah, here he comes."

3

Suzanne watched Dr. Edmund Grayson as he walked towards them, and her heart gave a tug when she saw how loosely his lightweight suit hung about his tall, spare frame. He looked weary, yet in spite of this, held himself erect.

The fine wrinkles around his pale blue eyes deepened into an expression of pleasure as he caught sight of his daughter, and the sadness about his mouth lifted as she put her arms about him.

"It's so good to be home again."

He kissed her cheek, emotion silencing him. He picked up one piece of luggage, Suzanne the other, and the three of them walked to the pale grey Mercedes.

Suzanne helped her father lift her things into the boot.

"Did they come with you to Heathrow?"

"Just Gramps. Gran's a bit poorly these days. Too many 'confusions' for her, she says."

"Sit in front with Papa, Suzanne," interposed Helene. "Tell us about the journey." She spoke quickly, the lilt of her French accent fondly familiar.

Suzanne's mind nicked gently over the

4

parting from her paternal grandparents. They had loved her being with them, she knew. When the time came for her to leave, her grandfather had insisted on making the long journey from Cornwall to Heathrow airport with her. He seemed reluctant to let her go . . . perhaps she might never see them again. She felt sad as she remembered all the goodbyes, and the tears in her grandmother's eyes. "What would you like to know?" she asked.

"Anything. Anything. Was the 747 full?"

"No. Only about a third . . . and most of those got off in Barbados. When we got to Trinidad the plane seemed almost empty."

"Did you have to wait long for this one?"

She shook her head. "Only about half an hour."

"Tired?" asked her father.

Again she shook her head. She was avid for news of home.

"Is Merle still here?" She said it quietly, afraid to betray her reason for asking.

5

"She returned to Martinique." Helene's reply came quickly.

"When?"

"Almost a year ago."

Suzanne's breath came fast. "And you never even wrote to tell me? Oh, Mother, how *could* you not tell me!"

Helene was silent.

"Did you see her before she left?"

"No. She just left."

"Didn't she even come over to say goodbye?"

Helene shook her head.

"Will she ever come back, do you think?"

"Who knows!" Helene shrugged her elegant shoulders.

"And Wim?" She said the name as casually as she could.

"He's well . . . so far as I know, that is. We haven't seen him for about two weeks."

Suzanne was conscious of her father's hands gripping the steering-wheel. His knuckles showed white. She scrutinised him carefully, noting how much whiter his hair was. "Poor Father," she thought. "He has lost so much weight." Yet her mind persisted in reverting to Wim. Finally, she said, lightly, "Oh, well, that's another one off Wim's list. It gives *me* a clear field again."

"Suzanne! Please do not say such things." Helene was shocked.

"Don't panic, Mother. I'm not serious. He always thinks of me as a child. . . anyway . . ." Then she changed the subject. "You haven't asked me about my exams. I got through them quite well. Six O-levels."

"We never doubted that you would, my dear," said her father. "Well done."

"And I suppose that is that," thought Suzanne, remembering all her hard study.

She turned to look out of the window, and as she watched the passing familiar scenes of childhood, her mind drifted back once again to the Cornish village of Pellisk where she had spent the past three years at school, going backwards and forwards, daily, from the County Grammar School to her paternal grandparents' home. They lived in a thatched cottage set in the middle of two acres of apple orchard. It was perched on the crest of a hill on what had been the old coach road to Falmouth.

The dormer window of her bedroom looked down across the few houses nestled at the foot of the hill and the creek where the swans had taken over. Each day when she got home from school, she would hastily devour treacle sandwiches, then take Sam the cocker spaniel for a walk, down to the creek. It was fun. Yet, however happy her memories of Cornwall were, they had never compared to the nostalgia she felt for Balandra . . . and now, here she was, home at last. Those three years away had seemed like a lifetime.

She opened the car window and drew in deep breaths of the scents she had missed so much. Dusk was falling fast and she could smell the burning charcoal used for cooking. Part of her young life, it reminded her of the glowing pieces of charcoal in the iron Adele used for pressing her dresses. *"Non, non,"* she would scold. "Musn't touch." Adele had been with them as far back as she could remember. She belonged to her past, just as Wim did.

All was quiet for a while, but as they

rounded a bend on the outskirts of St. Louis, Suzanne spoke again.

"Mother, shall we go shopping? I'd like to buy some new clothes. I've been saving my allowance. I've been looking forward to it."

Suzanne turned in her seat, her eyes searching her mother's face. She reached over and covered her mother's hand with her own. Helene looked up, giving a slow, wistful smile.

For a moment or two Suzanne kept her hand where it was, then gently withdrew it as she changed the subject yet again.

"You haven't asked me about my future plans yet, have you!"

But the remark was unheeded, and for the time being Suzanne was silenced.

Dr. Grayson switched on the headlights as they turned along River Road in the speeding dusk. The few shuttered shops grouped at the corner were deserted, and the shambling corrugated-iron dwellings threw weird shadows as the headlights of the car swept the unlit area. Their home in Spring Valley was three miles farther on. They left the tarmac and turned on to a rough track.

The Mercedes coped with the potholes as it had always done. A grader was used on the track once a year, but each rainy season it reverted to its original state of corrugation.

At last they were home. They turned into the jacaranda tree-lined driveway, Suzanne's senses alert to the wild clover-honey fragrance of the blossom. The headlights now revealed a vivid blue carpet of fallen petals on the grass and on the driveway.

About fifty yards farther on was the house.

The two-storey building was constructed on stilts about four feet above ground level and was built of red cedar against the ravages of the termite white ant. A wide veranda ran round the four sides.

For Suzanne's arrival, every light in the house had been turned on so that the trees and the surrounding shrubbery were illuminated. Large scarlet-studded poinsettia shrubs glowed bright, and cosmos daisies danced among the stolid clumps of brilliant orange and salmon pink canna lilies. Here and there were vermilion salvias, and against the house, large mauve blooms of thumbergia drooped from their hanging vines. Bougainvillaea, with its rainbow colours of paper-like blossoms, trailed the veranda supports.

Suzanne gestured appreciatively towards the garden, then turned and walked through into the spacious living-room.

"Oh, good," she said, aloud, as she looked about her, "nothing much seems to have changed."

The same flowered linen covers on the easy chairs and settees which faced the centre of the room where an oval table bore a crystal bowl of cut flowers. Soft beige rugs were placed at intervals on the polished red cedar parquet floor which extended on to the wide veranda.

Over against the wall on the far side of the room was Helene's mahogany desk, a piece of furniture she had insisted on bringing from France when she was a bride of sixteen. Above it hung an Arabian proverb, embroidered in coloured silks. Suzanne had learnt it off by heart when she was six years old . . .

He who knows and knows he knows,
He is wise, follow him.

He who knows and knows not he
  knows,
    He is asleep, wake him.
He who knows not and knows he
  knows not,
    He is a child, teach him.
He who knows not and knows not
  he knows not,
    He is a fool, shun him.

The words skipped through her brain as she remembered.

Her parents had followed her up the steps. Suzanne swung round and walked through to the kitchen.

Adele was preparing a salad and gasped as Suzanne appeared.

"Miss Suzy!" Her round brown face was wreathed in smiles. "And you so thin, eh . . ."

Suzanne laughed. "Aren't you pleased to see me, then?"

Adele clasped her hands fervently, then picked up the corner of her apron in her embarrassment, as if she expected to cope with tears.

"And what about Dudley?"

"He fine. Just fine." Adele giggled.

12

"I don't see him. Where is he?"

"Gone fishin' with that no-good brother a his. He do come and go all hours."

Helene appeared. She caught Suzanne by the hand and led her away upstairs.

"Mother!" exclaimed Suzanne, throwing her coat and bag on to the bed. She stood confused and was filled with a sense of vexation that the bedroom she had known and loved all her childhood had been completely stripped of familiarity. It was now furnished with turquoise chintz. The word "boudoir" raised itself in Suzanne's mind. But she said, "How pretty you have made it—but so . . . so . . . French." Then in a subdued tone, she added, "It's lovely."

"I have great plans for you, *chérie*," her mother continued, completely unaware of what she had swept away. "But we will talk of them another time. Now, see what a surprise I have for you."

Helene walked to the far end of the room and opened wide double doors to a walk-in wardrobe built entirely across the end wall. Suzanne could see a long row of new clothes and she groaned inwardly.

"Oh, but *Mother!*" The old sinking

feeling assailed her. "You *haven't* sent to Paris for those things, have you?"

"But of course. There is nothing in the shops here."

"But . . . but *Mother*, there *must* be. Madam Blanche had some wonderful clothes when I was at home before."

"Pouff! They are American. No chic, no fit."

"But I thought they were lovely."

"Perhaps you were too young to appreciate, Suzanne. You should know by now that there are no clothes in the world worth wearing except those that come from Paris."

"What a ridiculous thing to say," thought Suzanne. "Oh dear, oh dear, oh dear. Why can't I convince her that I want to choose my own clothes? She never gives up. Why won't she let me be myself? To choose what *I* want to wear . . . to make my own mistakes, perhaps . . . but to at least try. Surely it's not too much to ask. If only she could understand."

Helene walked across to the opposite corner of the room and opened white louvred half doors to display a new bathroom.

14

"It . . . it's gorgeous, Mother," said Suzanne. She felt swamped.

"I'm glad you like it, *chérie*," said Helene brightly, as she ran a practised eye over her handywork. Unexpectedly, she added, "Dinner is in half an hour, Suzanne. Don't be too long."

"I won't. Just a moment . . ."

Helene paused, half impatiently, as if she guessed what was coming.

"Mother, I want to know about Wim. Why did Merle go back to Martinique?"

"I really cannot tell you," she said, avoiding her daughter's eyes. "We'll talk about it tomorrow. Quickly now." Then she gave Suzanne a perfunctory pat on the cheek and hurried from the room.

Suzanne sighed. She walked slowly over to the rack of expensive clothes and carefully scrutinised them as though she knew beforehand what they would be like. She was unenthusiastic as she fingered one or two, yet as she came upon one which met with her approval, she selected it and laid it carefully upon the bed. It was an avocado green silk slip of a dress, perfectly cut. It was amazing how well her mother knew her measurements.

15

She gazed around the bedroom with its turquoise chintz drapes and elegant matching dressing-table, the silver-backed hand mirror and brushes. Then she walked over to her case and took out her old favourite ebony-backed whalebone hairbrush and guilty put it beside the silver ones. She pondered for a moment, then opened the top drawer of the new dressing-chest and slipped it inside.

She liked the bathroom. Everything was sparkling white except the black marble tiled floor and the rose-coloured soap and towels.

As she showered she thought how good it was to be home. Yet a cloud hovered on her horizon. How would her future shape itself? She felt unsure. She reached for a towel and dismissed her unpleasant thoughts as she stepped out of the shower.

Within half an hour, as her mother had requested, she walked through the living-room and out on to the veranda, wearing the dress she had selected from those of her mother's choosing and felt that everything was back to a point three years ago . . . already it was as if she had never been away.

16

2

THE sound of voices told Suzanne there was a visitor.

Tall and slim, she moved gracefully towards the veranda. She had piled her long, shining hair into a soft chignon. Her skin was clear, and so were her eyes. Intense blue and framed with luxuriant soft brown lashes.

Seated at the far end of the veranda she could see a young man in a white suit, immaculate against his polished brown skin. He was absorbed in conversation with her father, but as Suzanne walked towards them he rose, followed by Dr. Grayson, who made a hasty introduction.

"My daughter, Suzanne. Dr. Johnson . . . Ben." Then he left them, to pour drinks at the oval table where a silver salver bearing a selection of drinks had been set beside the flower arrangement.

Ben Johnson shook hands politely, but it was obvious to Suzanne that he was still concentrating on what her father had been

17

saying. He looked at her with a pair of serious brown eyes, giving her a searching approval. She smiled as his warm, brown hand gripped hers. His response was stimulating, though he remained so solemn that Suzanne would hardly have been surprised had he produced his stethoscope.

She looked around her with a slight feeling of shyness, relieved when her father returned with two sherries. He left them again to fetch one for himself, and as Suzanne sipped her drink she was aware that Ben Johnson was still regarding her thoughtfully. She smiled at him again and this time he grinned unexpectedly, presumably having put his medical problem aside for the time being. Her father, however, had other ideas, and the two doctors resumed their animated conversation about medical matters.

Suzanne excused herself on the pretext that her mother might need some help, yet knowing full well that she seldom needed help with *anything*. Helene was at that moment standing at the top of the steps, looking down the driveway, a far away look in her eyes.

The moon was full and the jacarandas

gleamed like filigree silver. A cool breeze moved across Suzanne's shoulders as she heard a car approaching.

She glanced at her mother. There was a look of rapt expectancy on her face. Suzanne felt dismay. She was disappointed that her first evening at home should have been made open house. Yet when she saw who the arrivals were her attitude changed.

"Oh! It's Claire and Vinny," she exclaimed, going quickly towards them.

A plump, ginger-haired woman struggled up the steps, clutching the skirt of her long, overtight flowered dress. Her friendly freckled face with its halo of unruly ginger hair proclaimed her generous outlook on life—particularly towards food. As she reached the top step she let go of her skirt and extended two well-developed freckled arms to enfold Suzanne against her ample bosom.

"You look stunning, honey!" she greeted, with a hug. "So . . . so Parisienne."

"I think she looks anything but French." Helene spoke abruptly, giving Suzanne a second and more critical

19

appraisal. To be outdone by her own daughter's charm was a new experience for Helene and she was not sure she was enjoying it.

"Hello, Vinny," welcomed Suzanne, as Vincent Landers followed his plump wife up the steps. "How are things?"

Vincent sidestepped his wife's taller and bulkier form and his face crinkled all over as it arranged itself into a sheepish smile. "Oh, so . . . so." He shrugged. "Goliath got out this morning and it took us the best part of the day to get him back into his stall. I think the cows were a bit disappointed."

"Who let him out?"

"God knows!" Vincent spread his gnarled hands and looked heavenwards, his wiry iron grey hair distinctly in need of a trim.

His slight figure had a crumpled pyjama look as though he was constantly grappling with his wife, but his weatherbeaten face belied any suggestion of being at a disadvantage. In company Vincent always appeared to be tagging along behind Claire, but this, Suzanne knew, was a pose. He and Claire were compatible to an enviable degree.

Their farm was situated in the hills well beyond Wim's coffee plantation, and they had lived there for thirty years. Claire was an American and Vincent had met her during a holiday in the United States. Having lived on the island for so long now, Claire had somehow acquired an odd, hybrid vocabulary which strangers found hard to place.

Vincent settled in a corner with a drink where no one would either notice or bother him. Yet he loved to watch others, happy in the knowledge that his wife always had enough social enthusiasm for both of them.

"Where's Wim this evening?" he heard his wife say. Her good-humoured face was flushed and she was all set to enjoy her evening.

"Oh . . . is Wim coming, too?" reacted Suzanne. Then noticing that her mother was still at the top of the steps, listening and gazing expectantly towards the shadows, she lowered her voice to a whisper. "Quickly, Claire, tell me. . . Why did Merle go back to Martinique?"

Claire looked at her pensively and seemed about to say something, but changed her mind, turning her head quickly in the direction of the veranda steps.

"What is it you would like to know?"

Suzanne heard the deep laughing voice with the Netherlands accent. She spun round and there was Wim van Branden, focusing her with his bright, fearless blue eyes.

Just over six feet tall, Wim van Branden's body was lithe though well covered, and it showed to advantage beneath his cream tussore suit. His unruly hair was sun-bleached and his skin tanned to a deep bronze.

As Suzanne observed him for that brief moment, something stirred within her—a chord of memory, perhaps. Memories of her early life came crowding in. As far back as she could remember, Wim had always been somewhere where she could reach him. Then her mind jumped to the present as she stammered, "I-I didn't know you were coming . . . Mother never said . . ."

Helene moved towards Wim. "Well, what do you think of her?"

Suzanne flushed. Why did her mother speak of her as if she was still a child?

"I am admiring her more as each moment passes." There was light irony in his voice.

A split second's embarrassment and Suzanne was reminded of his attraction. Her longstanding relationship with him was making her feel almost possessive, and it worried her.

Edmund Grayson came forward to hand Wim a whisky and soda. Wim, always gallant, raised his glass and said, "Here's to your return, Suzy." Then he added, "And to sweet seventeen."

The others echoed his words and Suzanne's composure returned. "Thank you, Wim. Thanks to all of you. It's good to be home."

Helene, happy in the knowledge that Wim had arrived, went through to the kitchen, pausing to regard her reflection in the gilt mirror. Her dark winged hair framed her high cheekbones, giving a perfect shape to her face. Her expressive full lips betrayed satisfaction with her appearance as she turned and walked on towards the kitchen. Her flame-coloured chiffon gown caressed her limbs as the gentle night breeze caught her movements.

Five minutes later she came back, clapping her hands. "Come, dinner is ready."

As they entered the dining-room it was obvious that Helene had put a great deal of effort into setting the scene. The antique walnut table was covered with a handmade lace tablecloth, an heirloom from her French grandmother. Deep salmon pink candles in silver candlesticks at each place setting, enhanced the pink and red roses in the white carved soapstone bowl. The sparkling crystal and the polished silverware made the whole table gleam in the candlelight which flickered intermittently from the cool breeze coming through the louvred windows.

"Ben," said Helene, "will you sit next to Suzanne?"

"I should be delighted."

"Have you been on the island long?" Suzanne asked, as Ben pulled out her chair so that she might sit. She noted that Wim was facing her across the table.

She heard Ben say, "No, not very long.

About six months. My home is Trinidad, though I've been away from it for some years now."

"You've been at medical school in England?"

He shook his head. "The United States. But I did a spell as a junior houseman in England—at the London Hospital for Tropical Diseases."

Suzanne watched the well-kept hands unfold his snowy napkin.

He looked up. "Your father tells me you have just finished your O-levels."

She nodded.

"What about A-levels?"

"No. It would have meant staying away even longer." She felt Wim's eyes on her and glanced across at him, but he looked away. She felt her colour rise and made an effort to appear casual, though whether she was succeeding she had no way of knowing.

Ben was questioning her again.

"I understand you were at school in Cornwall."

"Yes. Not boarding school, though. I attended the County Grammar. My grandparents' home was only about a mile away, so I was able to be with them."

"And you liked that?"

"Certainly." And for an instant her mind took her back yet again to her roomy attic with its dormer window, where on summer evenings she would climb out on to the roof and bask in the moonlight. But one didn't tell about such things. They were personal moments . . . as when the smell of the sun-warmed thatch mingled with the scent of honeysuckle and seeped into one's soul to remain there for ever.

Helene had prepared an excellent meal, as always. Entertaining was her special gift. This particular evening she had served mountain trout with crispy almonds, followed by grilled tenderloin steaks and a green salad. This was complemented by Suzanne's favourite dessert—cherries jubilee.

"Who's coming into the mountains with me?" Wim had finished his dessert and was leaning back in his chair, toying with a cigar. He removed the band, then absentmindedly slipped it onto his little finger.

"Why? Are *you* going?" asked Suzanne, interested.

"I might be. If someone would like to talk me into it." He looked across at Helene, but she dropped her eyes to her plate and concentrated on making sure her spoon was exactly dead centre.

Wim clipped the end of his cigar, then held it lightly between his teeth. Once more he looked across at Helene, but she kept her eyes down. He then struck a match and applied it to the cigar, repeatedly moving the flame first left and then right across the end of it.

Suzanne forced herself not to watch him. She turned to her father.

"Can you come with us?"

"I'm afraid not." He was so definite. He didn't even look up. "But perhaps Ben would like to keep you company. I should think the hospital could spare him for a few days."

Suzanne looked surprised.

Wim's cigar was now well alight and he held it passively, leaning forward and resting his arms on the table while the smoke from it drifted up through the candlelight in blue swirls. Now he was

27

looking across at Ben, who said, "I should like to go. Very much."

Helene took up the running. "That's four of us. Will you and Vincent come with us, Claire?" It was now obvious to everyone that Helene was only too delighted at the prospect.

"Shall we, Vinny?"

"Whatever you say, my love." He wagged his head.

"That's six of us," said Helene.

Edmund Grayson watched his wife's beautiful, animated face, but never once did she look at him. He was in no doubt that the prospect of the trip excited her. As always, it made him feel unimportant to her. He reached into his pocket and took out his pipe, filling it slowly but never getting around to smoking it.

Now and then Suzanne would look at her father, sensing his unhappiness. Why should her mother's high spirits upset him? Surely he could see she was enjoying herself. Suddenly the prospect of the trip into the mountains no longer appealed.

Ben was speaking. Suzanne turned to him. "Pardon?" She had to make an effort to bring her mind into focus. Ben repeated his question, but she did not hear what he was saying, even then, and for the time being he let it go.

Helene, Wim and Claire continued to discuss the proposed trip, and in deference to Suzanne, Wim asked her if she had anywhere special in mind that she would like to visit.

"Not really." Her reply was devoid of all enthusiasm.

Helene bit her lip. "I'll get some coffee," she said, anxious to divert attention from her disappointment.

They rose from the table and moved to the comfortable seats in the living-room. Ben followed Suzanne as she went across to the rail of the veranda. She looked out into the bright moonlit garden and then closed her eyes, giving herself up to listening to the crickets. When she opened them she found Ben studying her again. She shook herself a little and smiled. "Do you want any coffee?"

He shook his head. "Not particularly."

"Neither do I." She moved towards the steps. "No coffee for us, Mother. I'm going to show Ben the grounds."

Helene paused, coffee pot in hand, as

Suzanne picked out a few sugar lumps from the silver scuttle.

As Suzanne and Ben walked down the steps, he said, "Who's the sugar for? Me?"

Suzanne laughed. "You'll see," she said, shaking them in her cupped hands.

As they walked, Ben accompanied her with an old-fashioned courtesy and she warmed to him.

"Do you know that your father is considering retirement?" he asked.

"No, I did *not!*" Suzanne was disturbed. "Do you know why?"

"Not really . . . but I think, maybe, he's anxious to do a write-up on indigenous diseases. He has spoken about it from time to time. I know he finds it frustrating that his work never allows him sufficient time for it."

"I suppose I shouldn't be *too* surprised," said Suzanne, even more concerned. "I bet Mother is at the back of this. She's probably trying to persuade him to go back to France again—she has always had a bee in her bonnet about going back. She gets very restless sometimes, I know." She sighed. "Oh well, I suppose it's no good worrying. At the moment I simply cannot bear to think of anything except how good it is to be at home on the island again."

"I didn't mean to upset you."

"That's OK. I know you didn't."

They walked some distance without speaking, then Ben broke the silence by asking who Wim van Branden was.

"Oh, he's a plantation owner. Coffee."

"How well do you know him?"

She laughed. "That's a very good question." She paused. "He's like family. . . he's been around as far back as I can ever remember."

"Like an uncle, as it were?"

"No, certainly not like an uncle . . . oh, no. We argue too much for that. More like a big brother, I should think . . . at least . . ." But she never finished the sentence. She started to run towards some stables where a roan half-hunter was visible, his head protruding from his stall.

"Oh good!" she exclaimed. "Wim must have brought him back for me this morning." "I wish Mother had told me," she thought. "I could have thanked him sooner."

She reached up and stroked the horse's nose.

"Jason, meet Ben," she said.

Jason tossed his head and stamped impatiently. Suzanne patted him affectionately. "He was only a colt when I left," she told Ben. "I wanted to come and see him sooner, but I didn't know he was back. Anyhow, immediately I got home I was shoved in the shower and then in with the guests. I haven't had a chance to sort myself out yet."

"It sounds horrible." He grimaced.

She laughed. "So he has a sense of humour", she thought. "That's nice." Then she opened the stable door and led Jason out. He gave a loud whinny as she talked to him and patted his flank. Her spirits were rising. "Here, *you* give him the sugar."

Ben held out his hand to take the sugar lumps from her, and as it lightly touched her own she was aware of a pleasant sensation.

When they returned, the guests had departed. Helene had retired. Suzanne said goodnight to Ben and went upstairs.

Shortly afterwards she heard his car drive away.

She undressed and sat on the edge of her bed, wishing her mother could have come in and talked to her. "I suppose I shall have to go to *her.*" She sighed aloud.

She put on her bathrobe, going first down to the veranda where she knew her father sometimes sat and read for a while before retiring.

Pulling up a chair, she waited for him to speak.

"You didn't seem very keen on the trip into the mountains, after all," he said, cutting out preliminaries.

"It's only because *you* won't come. I've only just got home and I don't want to leave you again so soon."

"Your mother only wants to make sure there is plenty of interest for you. She has so looked forward to seeing you."

Suzanne sighed, thinking of all the new clothes and the expensive alterations to her bedroom. "I suppose so. But I do wish just the three of us could be together for a few days. Couldn't we?"

Edmund Grayson smiled. "We could go along the coast for a few days, if you like

. . . if it means that much to you. Just the three of us, I mean."

Suzanne brightened. "I'd love that. Tamarisk Bay?"

The doctor raised his eyebrows. "Um. *Must* we go somewhere so primitive?"

"Oh, please, Father. It would mean so much to me. You know I have always adored going there."

He paused. "You would be willing to go on the trip into the mountains later? Not to disappoint your mother?"

"Of course."

"Then I'll see what I can do." He patted her hand affectionately. "Now go and say goodnight to her."

For an answer, Suzanne stood up and then bent down to kiss his forehead.

Edmund Grayson reached for his pipe, lying beside him on the table. With his other hand he took his tobacco pouch from his pocket. Discovering that his pipe had already been filled, he now lighted it. Then he opened his book and continued reading for an hour.

Suzanne tapped on her mother's door.

"Come."

She walked over to her mother's bed and sat beside her. Gone was the chiffon evening gown. It had been replaced by a filmy nightgown in a soft shade of blue. Helene's eyes were large and luminous in the diffused lighting from the rose-coloured bedside lamp.

Taking Suzanne's hand, she said, "And how do you like Ben Johnson?"

"Nice," murmured Suzanne, somewhat absentmindedly. "Um, he's nice. Comfortable to be with." She hesitated. "Mother, are you going to tell me what happened? Or do I have to ask Wim myself?"

Her mother's eyes widened. She looked startled. "What, *chérie?*"

"Between Merle and Wim, of course," she replied, slightly impatiently. "I keep asking you, but so far you haven't given me a satisfactory explanation."

Helene looked down at the coverlet, pretending to straighten it. She lifted the magazine she had been idly reading, and as she put it on the bedside table, she said, lightly, "Don't try to make so much of it, *ma petite*. They weren't suited. That's all."

"How do you know? Did Wim tell you that?"

"Oh, I don't know. Somebody did. I can't remember." She affected a yawn, dismissing the subject.

Suzanne gave up. She realised by now that she would get nowhere with her mother in her present mood. She was very evasive about the whole thing. She would have to ask Wim himself.

Standing up, she said, "You're tired, aren't you?" then paused, thinking of something to say. "It was a lovely dinner party. The table looked beautiful."

"Thank you for that. You're the only one who said anything."

"You must have gone to such a lot of trouble. You never forget my favourite dessert, do you. It was delicious."

Helene twisted her shoulders. "Oh, well, I suppose I like doing these things. That has to be my satisfaction." Then she added, "Suzanne, why are you not keen on the mountain trip?"

"But I am. It's only because I've only just come home and don't want to dash off immediately without seeing something of

Father. Three years has been a long time, you know." She sat down again.

Suddenly her mother's arms were around her and Suzanne knew that she was crying. Gently comforting her mother, but wondering at the intensity of the tears, she felt constrained to ask questions.

She stood beside the bed for a few moments more, then kissed her mother tenderly and went quietly from the room.

Tomorrow she would ride over and see Wim.

3

SUZANNE awoke to the awaremess of long-remembered sounds. It was seven o'clock and full daylight.

She lay watching the rays of the sun filter through the flowered chintz drapes and listening to the keskedee bird. *"Faites vos jeux! Faites vos jeux!"* it kept repeating. She knew exactly where the fidgety small green bird would be—perched at the top of the highest oleander.

Then she heard the turn of the outside tap and the cascade of water into a galvanised watering-can. Dudley was about to tend the flowers which needed constant care, especially the roses and other European species her mother regarded as essential for a beautiful garden. She could hear no footsteps, but knew from the sound of trickling water that he was making his way from plant to shrub. She also knew that there was a sprinkler and a hose, but for some reason best known to himself he rarely used it.

Dudley had originally come from Barbados, and from his own account had run away from his domineering common law wife. For some years now he had enjoyed a liaison with Adele, and they seemed to have a good working relationship. Dudley's voice, with his rich Bajan accent, was like dark molasses, and when he laughed, the world seemed a good place.

Presently Suzanne heard the Mercedes start up. She went to the window just in time to see her father leaving for the hospital. She knocked on the glass to attract his attention, hastily undoing the catch, but she was too late. It had always been the same.

Still at the window, Suzanne looked up at the hills then down Spring Valley, after which the house had been named. Starting from a waterfall in the cleft of a rock, the stream gained momentum as it pursued its devious course down towards St. Louis. There it would tumble about in a dry river bed and get lost amid the stones.

In the early morning light, each blade of grass stood clearly defined against the trees that clustered about the cleavage.

Away to the east she could see the harbour. Fishing-boats coming in with the previous night's catch, yachts resting at anchor, and a steamship, probably a cruise vessel, which suddenly sounded its siren.

She sighed with contentment. Then moving away from the window shed her short flimsy nightgown to dance naked around her bedroom in pure delight at being alive.

She finally paused before the full-length mirror, running her hands over her young body, turning and posing. Throwing wide her arms, she pirouetted on tiptoe. "Ummm . . ." she said, aloud, "Ummm . . . not bad." Then as quickly as she had shed her nightgown she was into her jeans and open-necked blue check shirt, anxious to get to Wim.

Adele was already in the kitchen.

"Just orange juice, please, Adele. I won't be here for breakfast."

Adele shook her head in disapproval, but Suzanne laughed and caught at her apron to swing her round.

Adele giggled. "Now you done made me giddy, Miss Suzy."

"I dare say you'll get over it," called

Suzanne, already halfway across the small enclosed courtyard at the back of the house.

Adele shook her head, smiling and talking to herself as she continued what she was doing.

Suzanne's feet barely touched the ground as she ran through an archway to race across the levelled patch of ground towards the stables.

As she opened Jason's stall and led him out she felt a rush of gratitude towards Wim for caring for Jason whilst she had been away.

It had been Wim who had had the patience to teach her to ride. Her first mount had been a docile old pony long put out to grass. Wim used to call her Yvonne and then chuckle to himself. Suzanne never understood the joke. Yvonne's spine sagged so much Wim used to say she needed jacking up a bit, and then he would laugh again. And then they would both laugh, for no particular reason. Those days were fun.

It would have been pleasant, it occurred to her, to be able to remember shared childhood pleasures with her father, but even when she was very young he never seemed to be around. It had always been Wim.

She picked up each of Jason's feet for inspection before she heaved the saddle over his back. Then she mounted him and cantered across the clearing to the white picket gate which led out from the rear of the grounds onto the rough track leading to the hills.

Jason felt good under her as they made gradual upward progress towards Wim's plantation.

Set in the hills at about two thousand feet above sea level, he had built his bungalow on the lower slopes of his plantation, so that Suzanne knew she had about four miles to cover. Halfway up she dismounted and led Jason to a promontory so that she could sit on a favourite rock to survey the island from a vantage-point.

Some way out to sea, now, she could see the steamship moving towards the horizon, a turquoise and white ark on a calm sea. The harbour was still dotted with incoming fishing-boats, and the yachts, now that the steamship had departed, were left to their former quiescence.

But Suzanne's haste to see Wim permitted her to wait only four minutes before she remounted her horse to continue her journey upwards.

An hour later she turned into Wim's property between eucalyptus trees that lined the approach to his bungalow. As she rounded the bend she could see him standing at the top of his veranda steps, one hand against the support. His hair shone gold. Suzanne's, also, would soon lighten in the tropical sun.

"How did you know I was coming?" she called, riding right up to the foot of the steps before dismounting and patting Jason's head in her excitement at seeing him.

"I heard horse's hooves approaching from afar." He grinned.

Suzanne slid down from the saddle and led Jason across to a convenient tree and looped his reins over a branch. "You must have been waiting for me. You knew I'd come, didn't you!"

Wim merely smiled, his vitality enhanced in the early morning.

Suzanne climbed the steps and saw that his breakfast table was set for two. She took it for granted that it was for her. She sat down.

Maurice, Wim's manservant, appeared with a tray bearing steaming hot coffee and fresh baked rolls. The coffee, of course, from his own plantation.

"Good morning, Maurice." She knew him well, having spent many childhood days in the bungalow.

"Good morning, Miss Suzy. See you back, then."

She smiled up at him. "Yes, it's been a long time."

"Wait!" He raised a hand then vanished.

Suzanne's intuition told her that he would reappear with a slice of pawpaw. When it came, a slice of lime had been impaled on a long sliver of bamboo which was inserted into the fruit to resemble a sailing-boat, and the whole offering frosted with fine sugar. Maurice had always served it this way for her since it had delighted her as a child.

Wim waited for her to speak. "Well?" He raised one eyebrow, in that half-indolent way he had.

Suzanne started to say something,

44

stopped, then burst out, "What happened, Wim? Why did Merle go home?"

For some time he was silent, and Suzanne, unaware that she was trespassing, waited impatiently. Eventually he said, almost under his breath, "She lost interest."

"I just can't believe it! She adored you. What ever happened to make her go home?"

Wim looked down at his feet. A fleeting expression of annoyance crossed his face. Reluctantly, he said, "It was her own choice."

"But what happened? Is there someone else?" She waited.

Wim played with the spoon in his coffee-cup, then said firmly, "Don't pry, Suzy. There are some things you really should not concern yourself with. For whatever reason Merle left is *her* business. She is gone, and that will have to be the end of it."

Suzanne was dismayed. "I'm sorry," she said, humbly. "I didn't mean to pry." She felt the tears start but managed to blink them away.

There was a further silence. Finally, she

45

said, "Now that I'm home again, things aren't the same."

"In what way?"

"Well, for one thing, I'm worried about Father. He isn't happy. Not exactly unhappy . . . just, well, kind of defeated looking."

Wim looked serious as he gazed into the distance. "He has probably been working too hard."

Suzanne went on. "Then Mother. She seems all remote and funny. I just don't understand people any more. And now you. All my life you've . . . but even at this moment I no longer seem able to . . ." She stood up. "I'd better go."

"After coming all that way? Aren't you going to eat your pawpaw? Maurice will wonder what is wrong with it."

Slightly mollified, she sat down again. "Perhaps I am being over-sensitive," she thought, and tried a change of subject.

"Thanks for looking after Jason. He's in tiptop condition." She picked up the coffee-pot and poured herself a cup. "And you?" she offered.

Wim nodded. "Yes. If I leave it too long I mightn't get any." He gave a slow smile.

Suzanne felt the tension ease. "Oh, by the way," she said, lightly, "We're all going to Tamarisk Bay tomorrow."

"All?"

"The parents plus me."

"I see. Then you have spurned my offer to take you into the mountains."

"We didn't mean to do that. I'm sorry."

"That's all right. Perhaps we can go some other time."

At that moment a plantation buggy drew up. A fieldworker was at the wheel. He had an urgent query.

Wim ran down the steps and strode quickly towards the buggy and the man moved over as Wim climbed into the driving-seat. He waved absentmindedly in Suzanne's direction and she was left to finish her breakfast alone.

That same morning, when Helene awoke, it was ten o'clock. She had lain restless and sleepless for most of the night and then had fallen into a deep slumber about five.

Her mind went over and over her unhappiness, yet in between the pain of it she clung to thoughts of Wim. He had been her tower of strength for over twenty years now.

Wim had begged her, time and again, to leave Edmund and marry him, but there was the difficulty—she just hadn't the courage.

Edmund, though thoughtless of her need of his companionship, had been a good husband in his own limited way. He was kind, gentle and generous. His only fault lay in his obsession with his patients at the hospital.

From Helene's point of view he had no conception of her loneliness before she had known Wim. As a bride of sixteen she was bewildered at first when she was left for long periods on her own. If Edmund would have shared even one day a week with her she could have borne it, but even Sundays had been denied.

. . . And now her daughter was home again. She sighed, envious of Suzanne's youth and uncomplicated life at seventeen. Her thoughts drifted to her own childhood and how very different it had been from Suzanne's.

The huge rambling château in Provence where her family had lived for generations stood like a fortress in her mind's eye. Guarding her memories, calling her name and reaching out with its solid stone security to remind her that her spirit would for ever lie within its walls.

She recalled the beauty of the fields in summer, before the flowers had been gathered. And when they had gone, she thought about the wonderful leisurely late summer picnics. How her mother would pack a hamper and they would harness Bruno to the dog-cart and saunter through the grasslands surrounding the château until they reached one of their many favoured picnic spots. Time would stand still for them for a day.

The opening of the hamper was the most exciting part, and because Maman had made the filling of it an art in itself, Helene had been unconsciously influenced by that perfection all her life. It had quite naturally set her own standards, and she never offered less to her own family, even though she never really felt it was noticed. The snowy linen napkin wrapped around the bottle of red wine, the blue blanket overlaid with a spotless white damask tablecloth, the dainty gilt-edged china, silver cutlery—she could remember it all in detail as if it were only yesterday.

No food would appear until Helene had set the places correctly. Her brother Pierre's part was to release Bruno and do the lifting. And all the while Maman would sit waiting for the hamper to be set before her.

Then the moment would come when she lifted out the delicacies one by one, and patience became almost a game. Maman's smiles deepened with each succeeding dish, but they knew from experience that the last thing out of the hamper would be her special treat for dessert. Always something new and exciting. Their own tribute for all the trouble she had taken to please them was to be on their best behaviour, which was particularly conducive to a future occasion.

Helene sighed again as she thought of her mother. She was now seventy. Although frail physically, she was anything but frail mentally. Determined, hard working and very businesslike, she had carried on the family business when her husband died. Helene could only vaguely remember her father. He never figured very strongly in the picnic memories: she only knew that there didn't seem to be so many after he was gone.

Over the years Pierre had come to take his place, and it seemed to Helene that her mother had less and less time for her, busy as she was with the business and giving Pierre all the encouragement and guidance she could to preserve the family tradition: that of being one of the greatest perfume houses in France.

Helene held the thrill of business in her own veins, but her mother would never entertain such a possibility, and so only had time for Pierre. It was a bitter disappointment.

Then she met Edmund. She had been invited to spend a holiday in the French Alps with an English friend of her aunt's, and Edmund was a guest in the same house-party. He had been asked along at the last minute because he was at a loose end before taking up his appointment on Balandra.

Helene was intrigued with the strange, dedicated young man of twenty-eight who was destined to work on a far off island in the West Indies. It sounded so romantic.

Her interest in him was unexpected, even to herself, and it had been only a matter of days before Edmund in turn had fallen deeply in love with the vivacious young French girl.

Madame Pascale was not pleased. She did her utmost to prevent the marriage. "But you'll have Pierre, Maman. I should think you will hardly notice that I'm gone," she told her. She now bitterly regretted her unkind comment. Maman had probably known what was best for her. An arranged marriage would have meant she could have stayed in France.

When she got to Balandra she had not reckoned on being so homesick, and decided she must have been mad not to have found out more about it first. She was only sixteen then—now she was thirty-eight.

As the months went by Helene noticed that Edmund spent more and more time at the hospital. She began to get restless, and a feeling of dissatisfaction crept into her thinking. The day came when she desperately wanted Edmund to stay with her instead of going to the hospital. She begged him not to go, but either he didn't want to remain with her or he didn't understand just how desperate she was for his company. Her emotions rose within her, remembering.

It had been that same morning when Wim had come to the house very early, hoping to catch Edmund on some pretext, before he left for the hospital. Helene, piqued that her husband had gone in spite of her pleas to remain, and seeking company, had offered Wim breakfast. She knew it was wrong of her to do so, but she was hurt and angry, and anyway, Wim was fun to be with. She should have realised the danger.

Before she knew what she was doing she had confided in him.

His response had been enigmatic. She couldn't fathom his expression, even though he looked at her intensely. He remained completely silent. She was left wondering what he was thinking. Was his look one of sympathy? Or was it one of admonishment that she should have spoken of her husband in such a way, knowing that Wim was a friend to them both? Or was it something deeper? An indication that he had known of her restlessness for some time and was waiting for a sign? She knew he understood, but in that intense moment she had suddenly become aware of a deep response within her body and knew it for the answer she sought, yet had been completely unaware of such a thing until that moment. She looked away. Wim gently touched her hand, certain in his own mind that his meaning had been made clear to her.

But to Helene it was anything but clear. He had not even spoken . . . and then, some days later, when he had called on her again, she knew. She knew, as inevitably as a mountain descends to a valley, they would come together. It was merely a question of time.

Her second anniversary occurred a few weeks later, and to please her, Edmund had suggested an anniversary party. Wim would be among the guests.

At midnight someone had suggested thay all went for a picnic on the hills which stretched across the lower slopes beyond the van Branden estate.

The night was unusually chilly, in spite of the brilliant moonlight, and the wind on the hills was wild. They sought refuge in cars for warmth. Helene complained of feeling cold. She had forgotten to bring even a warm shawl.

"There is a blanket in my Ford," Wim had said. "I'll get it for you."

Then suddenly Helene found herself following him and would let no one prevent her. She turned towards the others, calling out against the wind, "We'll see you back at the house. Let's make it a race." She had climbed into Wim's Ford without a qualm. The champagne must have gone to her head. She remembered leaning back against the seat, contented and sleepy. When she awoke the Ford was parked beside the track and Wim was beside her, still as a statue and looking at her.

"What's the matter? Why have we stopped?" She smiled at him. There was a question in her eyes.

"We shall be in trouble with the others," he said, not really caring.

"Then why don't you drive on?" she challenged.

He still didn't move.

"Don't you care?" she said, still smiling at him with her dark expressive eyes.

Suddenly he was serious. "Helene . . ." He pulled her towards him along the bench seat, blanket as well. Then she was in his arms and he was kissing her and holding her so tight she could hardly breathe.

For a moment or two he relaxed his hold yet continued to cradle her as she rested against him contentedly. His hand sought the softness of her cheek and the line of her neck beneath her fragrant hair.

"We must go back," she whispered, "or it won't stop at this."

"Do you want to?"

Shaking her head gently she pulled his hands away and moved back, gathering the blanket about her.

Wim reluctantly switched on the ignition and the headlights and they drove home in silence, Helene's thoughts churning, her body in suspense.

The following day, after a sleepless night, Helene drove over to the plantation.

Wim's father had gone to St. Louis on business and Wim was waiting for her as if he knew she would come.

That morning was etched in her memory for ever. She remembered every

56

detail with clarity . . . coasting to the foot of the steps in the small red Fiat she had then owned, shifting the gear into neutral and pulling on the handbrake which needed oiling.

Wim, strong hands loosely forward and resting on the veranda rail, moved casually towards her. As he left the shade the predatory sun played on his young blond head. He came across to the small car and rested a hand on its roof.

Helene removed her sun specs, opened the car door and Wim waited for her to get out. He closed the car door after her and they mounted the steps together, the tenuous cord of desire pulling taut between them. It stretched into pain.

They entered the cool, long room with its leather upholstery and well-stocked bookshelves. It was a very masculine room. A bar had been built across one corner.

Helene crossed to the bar and climbed on to a stool. Wim walked behind it and placed two glasses on the polished oak, then went through to the kitchen to fetch ice. When he returned he poured two long lime and sodas, and as he handed her one of them she took it with trembling fingers.

Wim merely sipped his own drink. His eyes never left Helene. The message in her eyes was unmistakable.

He went through to the kitchen again and instructed Maurice on an errand, then locked the rear door. When he turned, Helene was standing in the doorway. He walked past her and she followed him. He opened the door to his own bedroom, and when they were inside he locked that also.

Helene came towards him, holding out her arms. Wim grasped them just above her elbows and held her fast. Drawing her arms tight against her sides and gathering all his strength into his hands, he shook her. Shook her until her teeth chattered and her fair fell down over her eyes. Her face went white as his fingers held her like iron bands and he was breathing hard.

"You shouldn't have come," he said, in a hard, strained voice. Then he let her go, turning his back on her. He walked away towards the window, gazing blindly at the bamboo blinds which had been lowered to keep out the sun.

Helene was completely at a loss. It was

impossible for her to fathom his motive for the cruelty he was inflicting on her when she had come to him with love in her heart.

Then swiftly her mood changed and she ran at him, beating him with her fists.

He turned and struggled with her, now trying not to hurt her. He grabbed her hands and held them while she fought to free herself, sobbing and catching her breath with fury. He threw her on to the bed with such force that it winded her. She lay back, panting as her breath came in gasps. "I hate you for this. I'll. . . I'll . . ."

"What? What will you do?" His anger mounted. "Show your bruises to your husband? And then tell him how you got them?" He paused, taking a deep breath and fighting his emotions . . . emotions that were new to him.

Helene buried her face in the pillows. *His* pillows. To think she had put herself in this terrible situation. It was unbearable. She sobbed uncontrollably.

Suddenly Wim was beside her, his arms around her and holding her so tight she thought she would suffocate.

And then it was Wim who was trembling. He held her ardently, caressing her and kissing away her tears. And soon, no matter how he had hurt her, the primitive female in her responded to his lovemaking.

Then came the stillness, those enchanted moments when time seems eternal. They slept, stirring once to rediscover each other. Again they slept, and when Helene awoke it was noon. Wim was no longer beside her, but she had no need for conjecture.

She went into his bathroom. The hot shower, then cold, eased her bruises. She examined her arms. They already showed black and blue marks where his fingers had gripped her. But she smiled, fingertips exploring the throbbing pain with gratification. The bruises would soon heal, and the ache would go, but now, so long as she lived, the memory of that moment of surrender would remain with her.

When she was dressed she found Wim on the veranda, lounging in a cane chair with his feet up on the rail and his unfinished drink beside him.

"I must go," she said. It sounded matter-of-fact, but it was not how she felt.

He stretched out an arm and drew her to him. "Not yet."

"I must. Edmund may be back."

He walked with her to the car.

Two months later she had discovered she was pregnant.

Helene gave a deep sigh, dragging her thoughts to the present.

When Edmund had made his request— that the three of them might have a few days at Tamarisk Bay, she could not bring herself to refuse, even though she relished the prospect very little. If their plans meant so much to them it was the least she could do to fall in with them. Edmund asked so little of her. Besides, there was the trip into the mountains to look forward to.

She thought about Tamarisk Bay. It was very hot there, humid too, and she hated too much humidity. The mountains, at three thousand feet, were much more an attractive proposition. Not only that, Suzanne would be sure to want to stay at that squalid little beach hotel where she went as a child with that Howard family and their brood. She never did stop raving about it. Oh well, she supposed she would have to make the best of it.

Her thoughts turned again. This time on what clothes she would take with her.

There was a knock on her door. It must be Suzanne.

Suzanne rode slowly home. She had an uncomfortable feeling. Her visit to Wim had been very disappointing. Inconclusive. She felt depressed.

She stabled Jason and walked back to the house, flicking lightly at the grass with her riding-whip.

When she came to the rear veranda she could hear the telephone ringing. It was Ben Johnson.

"I've been given time off to take you to lunch," he said.

"What are you? The entertainments committee?"

He didn't bridle. "If you like," he replied.

Suzanne frowned, then remembered his friendliness the previous evening. "What time, and where?" she replied.

"One o'clock in the foyer of the Mirador?"

"Yes. That will do nicely. I can do my shopping first." She did her best to sound enthusiastic.

"I shall look forward to seeing you," Ben said.

Suzanne replaced the receiver. "I must go in and see Mama," she thought, walking slowly up the stairs and along the corridor to tap lightly on the door.

"Come."

Suzanne entered apprehensively, but her mother smiled as she approached the bed.

"I'm just off, Mother. Ben Johnson is taking me to lunch at the Mirador."

"Oh, good."

"I'll be back about three. May I borrow your car?"

"If you like. I presume you can drive."

"Of course. I took my test in England. I wrote and told you. Don't you remember?"

"I'd forgotten. Yes, you did." Helene's brow clouded. "Did you see Wim?"

"Yes."

"Well. Did you find out what you wanted to know?"

Suzanne shook her head. "He didn't seem particularly pleased to see me."

"You are imagining things. Of *course* he was."

"I don't think so." She played with the scarf on her hair, retying it as if to convince herself she was correct in her assumption and yet not wanting to believe it.

"You were lucky he was there."

"He seemed to be expecting me. The table was laid for two."

Her mother made no comment and Suzanne felt at a loss, inclined to instant withdrawal. She backed towards the door. "I'll be back about three."

"Take care, *chérie.*"

But Suzanne made no rejoinder.

In the lobby of the Mirador Hotel Ben Johnson was waiting beside the gift kiosk, idly studying the display. He had been there for fifteen minutes, but Suzanne made no apology for being late.

They walked into the Grill Room just in time to get a secluded corner.

"What will you have, Suzanne?"

"I'm not very hungry. Just a salad, please."

64

"Your father told me to give you a *good* lunch."

"Don't fuss. I get enough of that at home," she replied, rather sharply. She felt impatient.

The memory of her visit to Wim was still with her, and try as she might it would not go away. There was something she didn't understand. Something that eluded her.

Having suffered a slight setback, Ben waited until she spoke again.

"Did my father tell you that we are going to the coast?"

He nodded. "Just for a few days, he thought."

"Yes. We can go on the mountain trip when we come back." Then she added, as an afterthought, "I'm glad you're coming with us."

Ben pressed his hands together, effecting humility. "You are most kind."

They both laughed.

"Sorry, I didn't mean to sound patronising."

"You didn't."

The waiter came over and handed them

the menu and left them while they made a choice.

"What is amusing you now?" Ben folded his arms.

"The menu. You'll have to read it for me—it's all in French—and French irritates me."

"I should have thought French was a natural language for you."

Suzanne pulled a face, then shook her head. "'Fraid not."

"But your mother . . . she taught you French, surely."

"She tried to, but I seem to have an inborn aversion to it."

They had almost finished their lunch when Suzanne caught sight of a couple across the room. They were just getting up to go.

"What is it?"

"Don't look now, but I've seen that girl before . . . She was on the plane."

"How can I know who you mean if I don't look up?" Ben discreetly raised his eyes to where the couple were occupied in leaving the table.

"Isn't she gorgeous," Suzanne whispered.

"You mean her red hair?"

"Ben! How can you! It's the most beautiful auburn colour."

Ben shrugged. "Not my type, anyway. I thought pretty girls were supposed to be jealous of one another . . ."

"How could anyone possibly be jealous of a girl like that?"

"Looking at the situation medically . . ." began Ben, putting his head on one side and studying the girl at a distance.

"Well?" Suzanne turned to him.

"She looks far from well, to me," he went on.

"How can you possibly tell at this distance?"

"Easily. By the way she moves, for one thing."

They watched the couple leave their table and make their way to the exit.

Suzanne gave a theatrical sigh. "*I* think she is unhappy."

"Oh, and what leads you to that conclusion?"

Suzanne leaned her elbows on the table and rested her head on her hands. "Because the two of them were sitting across the gangway from me, and during the whole flight she hardly opened her eyes, let alone spoke, even to the man she was with." Suzanne remembered, also, how attentive the man had been, and wondered what the relationship might be.

When Ben didn't reply, Suzanne looked at him, but his expression was inscrutable. "To get back to us," he began.

But Suzanne cut him short by glancing at her watch and saying, "Goodness, I must be going. I've got lots to do yet, before tomorrow."

Ben was disappointed. The lunch date had been much too hurried for his liking. As they left the Grill Room he had to almost run to keep up with Suzanne. They got as far as the door when he remembered he hadn't paid the bill and had to turn back.

"Thanks for the lunch," Suzanne called over her shoulder. "See you when we come back from Tamarisk Bay."

Five minutes later Ben climbed into his Pinto. He sat thoughtfully for a while before reluctantly switching on the ignition. Somehow the day didn't seem quite so bright.

4

THE Graysons were fast approaching Tamarisk Bay. Their journey to the western tip of the island had taken them on a winding course across the lower slopes of the mountains and they were now descending through peripheral areas of a once cultivated spice plantation. Now the nutmeg and cinnamon trees had reverted to their wild state and could be seen amongst wild fruit trees and ferns.

Tall trees with dense foliage and drooping vines made the going dim, and Edmund Grayson switched on his headlights to see his way through the eerie adandoned terrain. The deepening silence exaggerated the sound of the car engine, and the intense humidity didn't please Helene. She opened her vanity case and took out some cologne. Suzanne put her head out of the window: she found the warm exotic fragrance intoxicating.

Soon they came to a clearing and the scenery changed. They passed through a small village where patches of bananas and breadfruit trees were interspersed with tall silky-tasselled Indian corn and bare compounds of earth where children, naked except for perhaps a vest, played on the sun-baked soil with not a care in the world.

About six or seven miles further on, Edmund Grayson took a right turn and began the slow progress along a track through tropical undergrowth towards their destination at the edge of the sea. The narrow path twisted and turned through another small settlement, with chickens, pigs and goats darting about in terror as of necessity he had to maintain his pressure on the horn.

Suzanne glanced at her mother and saw her lips tighten. But merriment was bubbling up inside Suzanne and she had to fight to keep her mirth under control.

They finally drew up in a clearing at the back of some sand dunes, dwarf palms either side of the way down to the self-contained dwellings. They were euphemistically referred to as cottages, but were spartan in the extreme. Yet in spite of this they had a certain charm.

Strategically dotted about the dunes, each one enjoyed its own privacy and view of the ocean, connected as they were by a series of hidden pathways through a profusion of tropical plants. Uphill and downhill they went. It was impossible to count the dwellings at one sweep of the eye. There were about thirty, but many of them were impossible to see even from the beach.

At the top of the slope to the left was a small office where the husky, bearded manager was standing in the doorway, holding a snorkle and flippers in his hand. As Edmund approached him he walked over to hang his equipment on a hook. In a basket beside the door was a freshly landed ray almost three feet in diameter. Its whip-like tail with the poison barb was thrashing in desperation at the still embedded harpoon. Helene shuddered.

Suzanne gazed out towards the coral reef where the breakers were foaming with the receding tide. On the beach, as far as she could see, was the silver sand she remembered so well. Tall, shady trees grew almost down to the water's edge.

The manager welcomed Edmund and

chatted for some time as if he were an old friend. Helene stood waiting with impatience.

"It's so humid, Edmund," she complained, as he returned to her, formalities completed. "I must have a shower." Her head was aching and the journey against her inclination had wearied her.

"Of course, my dear. And a rest before lunch." He glanced down at her feet and noticed she was wearing high-heeled shoes. He pointed to them with concern, saying, "I'm afraid you will have to wear flat heels while we are here, Helene. Your ankles may swell if you don't."

"Oh, rubbish! You fuss over me too much." She was getting more and more irritable. It was difficult walking down the slope on the damp sand and she hated him because he was right. Doctors were impossible. They noticed everything.

Suzanne glanced quickly at her parents. Whatever was wrong with her mother? Her father always tried to do his best for them and yet she had often known her mother to act like this.

In an effort to divert their attention she

pointed to the colony of weaver birds flying in and out of their nests which were suspended from branches on long trails of grasses. The nests swayed unpredictably with the feverish activity. "Just look at those birds," she said. "They are still here —chattery and squabbly as ever."

But no one answered her. She tried again. "Shall we have a swim later on when the sun isn't so hot?"

"Perhaps," said Helene, abruptly.

Realising there was not much more she could do to ease the tension, Suzanne ran towards the beach, carrying her own case. With a final effort at gaiety she swung round. "See you at lunch!" But her parents had already turned away. A little farther down the path she paused and looked up. She could just see them walking to their cottage, their heads bobbing in and out of view until they finally disappeared among the coral rocks which were covered by feathery tamarisk trees and cascading bougainvillaea, growing indiscriminately from sandy crevices.

She finally reached the beach and turned right for about fifty yards to enter cottage number ten where she had stayed on her previous visit, now ten or twelve years ago. Where have those years gone, she wondered.

The cottage was just one barely furnished room, except that it did have a minute dressing-room behind it which sported a row of pegs on the wall. There was no covering on the coral block floor and the only furniture was a single bed with a mosquito net suspended from a hook in the ceiling and a washstand bearing a large jug of water standing in a basin. A small china soapdish, with a perforated lid for the soap to rest on, completed the assemblage. Suzanne thought it was bliss.

She remembered how at night she had listened to the sea as she lay within the security of her mosquito net. The windows were just large apertures with expanded metal guards against possible intruders— by animals rather than humans.

She looked around. The printed cotton curtains in blue, yellow and red were the same ones as before. They had been washed, no doubt, but looked as if they were about to fall apart. She would have to pull them gently. Still no electricity. Tilley lamps or candles were still used for illumination.

Suzanne put her case on the bed and opened it to take out her swimsuit. She changed into it as fast as she could and put on plimsolls: they would protect her feet from the blistering hot sand at midday.

She ran down to the sea with abandon, to swim in the warm water, knowing that her parents would not miss her for a while. No doubt her father would be doing his best to placate her mother.

Helene sat on one of the beds and reluctantly removed her high-heeled shoes. "I really cannot think why Suzanne insists on coming to this awful place. There are plenty of good hotels."

"Let's humour her this time, Helene. Her memories of home have had to sustain her during her three years away. She loves this island as much as I do. Let's not spoil it for her."

His wife was silent.

Edmund had ordered some cold drinks, and by the time they arrived, Helene had showered in the adjoining unit and was resting on her bed with the window curtains drawn. She looked happier. Theirs was one of the few cottages with an integral shower and toilet. Most guests had to walk to the main toilet block.

Edmund poured his wife a long cold drink with plenty of ice and placed it on her bedside table. She caught hold of his hand. "I'm sorry," she whispered.

He bent down and kissed her forehead, his hand touching her hair. "You're cooler now. That's better. I understand." His eyes were compassionate.

But Helene felt mean. She was really sorry she had been so irritable with him. Guilty too, as always. As she watched him undress she thought of Wim and how tangled her emotions were. It's all Wim's fault, she tried to convince herself, but knew it to be untrue. It was something within her own personality that she could not adjust. Taking it out on those she loved would not help her. How I despise myself, she moaned inwardly.

Edmund came out from his shower, smelling fresh and clean with his hair still damp. He looked quite boyish. Something melted inside her. "Turn the key," she said, quietly.

Edmund looked at her with some surprise, but walked over to the door and did as she bid him. She held out her hand to him, then moved over to make room for him on her bed. He slipped off his towelling robe and lay down beside her. As he put his arms around her she kissed him and drew closer to him, trying, as he held her, to push all thoughts of Wim from her.

But Edmund's ardour had long since been extinguished. Yet he remained with her in an effort to comfort her, and some time later her long dark lashes covered her luminous brown eyes and she slept.

Edmund carefully eased himself off her bed and walked over to his own, where he lay down pensively. He had that old feeling again: it was a deep disquiet.

The dining-room was large and airy, being completely open along the two sides against the beach. Thatched with banana palm, the roof well overhung to meet the eventuality of tropical rain. The large kitchens were beyond the solid walls on the other two sides.

At the corner of the building nearest the beach an inverted tin was secured to a pillar just below roof level and a length of stick wedged between the stays. It was the gong for summoning guests to meals. The stick would be taken out and inserted upwards into the tin and waggled until it made an inescapable din. Suzanne recalled how she had vied with the other children for the privilege. The sound was so loud that it carried to a distance of at least a mile each way.

There was an outside veranda running the whole length of the dining-room parallel with the shore. This was where long cold mid-morning drinks were dispensed, and before lunch and in the evening it served as a bar.

The main buildings had electricity, run off a small generator that grumbled in the distance. The lights were never very bright and often flickered, but no one (except Helene!) expected up-to-the-minute efficiency: that was part of the charm of the place.

On the other side of the main pathway was a large open-sided lounge, also thatched with banana palm, with sturdy canvas-covered furniture. Sitting there in the heat of the day Suzanne could smell the warm dampness. Even the sand. Intangible yet pungent, the humid, mildewed fragrance was forever a haunting memory of the carefree days of her childhood. The place had a primitiveness that stirred her deeply.

Beyond the lounge were the other cottages, just a few, including number ten. In front, growing out of the sand, were the shade trees the weaver birds inhabited. The beach and the ocean lay beyond, deserted for most of the day. But it was there always . . . inviting . . . beckoning . . . like a friend or lover who offers paradise.

As Edmund handed the menu to Helene she gave him a searching look. Though his eyes met hers only briefly she hoped that she had been forgiven.

As for Suzanne—she was munching a piece of melba toast, thankful that her mother's mood had improved. Her youthful enthusiasm had turned to food. She could smell the same delicious soup as before—a kind of julienne they always made.

She had put on a new fine cotton dress she had bought in Madam Blanche after having lunch with Ben the day before . . . just yesterday. It was American made, with no shoulder straps, and was kept up by the shirring on the bodice. Cleverly cut on the bias, the skirt spread out into fullness, yet with a slender waistline. Suzanne was pleased to notice that her mother was wearing flat sandals as her father had recommended. She must have brought them with her, she surmised.

It was almost the end of the meal. Suzanne was peeling an orange and her table napkin slipped to the floor. As she was about to pick it up her mother said sharply, "Leave it, Suzanne."

A masculine voice said, "Please, allow me," and Suzanne found she was looking straight into a pair of mock-serious grey eyes. It was the young man from the night who had accompanied the girl with the sad face.

He picked up the napkin and handed it to her.

Suzanne felt her heart give a rapid beat. "Thank you." It did not sound at all like her own voice.

"Paul Raymond, m'am." He made a formal bow. "And may I introduce my sister Erica?" He stepped to one side as the tall elegant girl appeared.

Travelling in the aircraft, the long chestnut hair had been confined beneath a silk scarf. Now it was hanging loose, and very beautiful. Gone, also, were the dark glasses, so that Suzanne could now see her eyes. They were an unusual shade of hazel and flecked with gold. She was wearing a white caftan with wide bands of embroidery at neck and sleeves.

"We have only just arrived." Erica's voice was husky and she had a leisurely way of speaking.

"So have we," said Helene. "But whatever made you come to a place like this when you could have stayed at a decent hotel farther along the coast?"

Paul laughed. "We much prefer somewhere like this. Somewhere off the beaten track."

"How did you get here?"

"We hired a car."

Suzanne addressed Erica. "Are you feeling better?" She said it without thinking.

A small frown creased Erica's smooth brow. "Better?"

"I-I'm sorry. I thought you felt poorly on the journey."

"Oh dear! Was it that obvious? Yes, I didn't feel too good, as a matter of fact."

Paul put a protective arm about Erica's shoulders. "My sister has been very ill," he said. "She has only just come out of hospital."

Erica looked away and Paul smiled at Suzanne, hoping to quell her embarrassment. She was plainly sorry to have made the personal remark.

"Perhaps we shall see you later," he added.

"Perhaps meet for a drink before supper," suggested Helene.

"A very good idea," Paul replied. Erica turned to smile at them as they passed on to their own table.

Five idyllic days had passed.

Suzanne immersed herself in the pleasure of being with her parents again, and unexpectedly, she had found that Erica sought her company. This gave her a great deal of pleasure as she had thought at first that Erica might have been offended over her thoughtless remark.

Paul was inclined to spend his days with the two girls, when in fact, both would have liked to be able to exchange confidences, without Paul as an audience. But it was not to be. Erica explained that he had left his business, for her sake, to bring her on the holiday because she had been so low in spirits after an unhappy love affair. Suzanne quite understood his point of view and that he would want to remain protective, but was curious about Erica's unhappiness.

One day, when they were sitting on the beach and Paul was swimming not too far away, Erica confided in Suzanne. It was, she said, a case of the old, old story. She had fallen in love with a married man. But, there was a difference—she had been completely unaware that he was in fact married. The man she loved had led her to believe that he was free.

Suzanne didn't know quite what to say.

Eventually, she asked, "Do you still love him?"

Erica shook her head. "How can I? That sort of deception kills love. I think if two people love each other they should at least be honest—even if there are bad things—they should know of them. It's much easier to face than finding out in a round-about way.

Paul was walking towards them. "My goodness! You two look serious." He was back with them again, and in spite of themselves they couldn't help laughing. He was like a small boy standing there hoping to be noticed.

That night when Suzanne went to her cottage, she undressed and put on a cool white cotton nightgown trimmed with a deep flounce of broderie anglaise. It was perfect for the tropical night.

She locked her door and pulled back the faded curtains and climbed under her mosquito net. For a while she sat hugging her knees and gazing out at the glorious night sky with huge stars and an almost golden moon that dipped its reflection into a shining pathway to the horizon.

At last Suzanne lay down. At first she

thought about Erica, who certainly hadn't deserved to be deceived by an unscrupulous man. But after a while her thoughts went to Wim. Dear, kind, straightforward Wim, whose integrity was never in doubt. As she lay there thinking about him she was beset by unfulfilled longings. Was it only a few days ago that she had once again heard his deep laughing voice behind her as he arrived unexpectedly at the house?

All her childhood memories came flooding back . . . memories of Wim and the good times they had shared. She knew his bungalow even better than her own home . . . and then, when she had only just come home from school in France she learned she was to be sent back to Europe again to finish her schooling. She had been furious with her parents and had gone over to beg Wim to intercede with them on her behalf. But he wouldn't. He actually agreed that it was best for her. She had hated him for that, accusing him of wanting to be rid of her. And when she new into a tantrum he had merely laughed at her.

. . . And so she had gone to Cornwall

to attend the local grammar school, living with her paternal grandparents.

But what now. . . ? Would Wim ever come to know how much she loved him?

With a sigh of longing she closed her eyes at last and fell into a deep, satisfying sleep. They were going home tomorrow.

The morning's departure proved worrying. Dr. Grayson was feeling unwell.

When Helene questioned him he was evasive, and she became somewhat impatient.

"Can you not tell me what is wrong, Edmund?"

He shook his head.

"Have you a pain anywhere?"

"Just a small one."

"Where?"

"It's probably indigestion. Will you hand me my case. I have some pills in it that might help."

Helene opened the case and the doctor selected a small white pill and put it in his mouth. The bottle went into his pocket.

Suzanne was alarmed. "Is there anything I can do to help?"

"Yes, my dear. I'd like you to drive, if

you will. Just part of the way. I'll be fine a bit later on."

And so the incident passed.

Suzanne drove for an hour and then Dr. Grayson took the wheel, apparently recovered.

Helene grumbled at him for eating his breakfast too fast, but Suzanne was much more concerned. She suspected the pain was not indigestion but something more serious.

The journey home went fairly well from then on, but Suzanne remained worried about her father.

Her thoughts then turned back on the few days holiday and the friendship that had come about with Erica. Erica and Paul had promised to contact them as soon as they returned to St. Louis, and Helene had asked them if they would like to come with the others into the mountains. Suzanne was surprised that Helene could extend such an invitation without consulting Wim, and wondered how he would react.

When they reached the house, Ben Johnson was there to greet them.

Dr. Grayson had hardly removed their

luggage from the car before he questioned Ben about the hospital. The mundane query provoked his wife.

"Can you not give the hospital a rest until tomorrow, Edmund? Let us at least get into the house first."

Dr. Grayson was silent.

"Have you all enjoyed your holiday?" Ben filled the silence.

"It was great," said Suzanne. "I could have stayed for ever."

Ben laughed. "I'm glad you didn't."

Suzanne was pleased.

"Oh, by the way," Ben continued. "Mr. van Branden wants you to let him know when you are ready to go into the mountains. He says he has everything organised."

Dr. Grayson was lost in agitation. He *must* get back to his patients. Trips into mountains meant nothing to him.

5

IT was seven o'clock in the morning ten days later that Vincent Landers was sitting patiently in his Range Rover. In fact, he had almost fallen asleep again. He was waiting for his wife.

The Range Rover was loaded with all their gear and, in Vincent's opinion, far too much of it. Not that he wished to challenge Claire's needs. She might argue, merely because she loved a tussle of wills. But, unfortunately for Vincent, she was never keen to quit the arena. Anyway, he told himself, it was much too hot to argue.

Claire finally emerged. Her jacket and slacks bulged in all the expected places. They had not been worn for several years but she was determined to dress for the occasion.

Her face had been creamed as a protection against the sun, and atop her unruly ginger hair was a pith helmet which she had dug out from the back of a cupboard.

She came waddling towards the Range

89

Rover, hopefully making an attempt to climb into it. Vincent gallantly left his driving-seat, and walked round to the other side of the vehicle and gave her a shove which almost knocked her hat off.

"Thanks, love. You didn't have to overdo it!"

They both laughed good-naturedly. Claire had long lost her vanity. It was a side to her character that endeared her to her family and friends.

"Are we late?"

"Yes." Vincent grinned, putting her at her ease. "But I guess they'll wait for us."

It was about fifteen miles to Wim's plantation and they arrived to find the others already assembled.

Wim's bungalow was built on a rise, with two garages beneath the veranda which extended the whole width of the front of the building. Split bamboo blinds were rolled up and secured.

On the veranda, floral-patterned cushions were scattered in the rattan lounge chairs which had feet rests. Low, glass-topped rattan tables were placed beside them.

A cheer went up as the Landers' Range Rover crunched to a halt.

Wim came to greet them, looking handsome in his dark blue jacket and slacks, his strong body showing beneath the denim.

"Good morning, all," he grinned, his blue eyes raking over the contents of the vehicle as if he expected more than two people to be in it.

Claire, perfectly aware that he was teasing her, held out her hand to him for help as she clambered down for him to inspect her outfit. But his grin merely widened, his white even teeth shining against his sunburnt face.

The three walked towards the others, then Wim went back to supervising the stores and other baggage.

Helene stood apart from the others. Wim sensed she was watching him and he turned. As their eyes met a knife turned inside her and she looked away.

Suzanne went towards him with her camera. "Wim, can you fix this for me? It won't seem to click back properly." She pointed to the defect and he took it from her carefully. With seemingly little pressure he corrected the fault and handed it back to her, smiling at her as he did so.

Helene felt a stab of jealousy. It is ridiculous to be jealous of my own daughter, she thought irritably. Both Wim and Suzanne felt her intense gaze upon them and turned to question her with their eyes.

"Are you all right, Mother?"

Helene moved towards Suzanne, and looked with distaste at the girl's faded blue jeans and T-shirt. "Where is your hat, Suzanne?"

"My hat?" Suzanne gave a puzzled frown. "I don't need a hat, Mother."

"I wish you to wear one. Go and find one."

Suzanne was startled by her mother's tone. She had spoken to her as if she were a child. Surely she hadn't forgotten how old she was. However, she went obediently to find some headgear—it would never do to upset her mother before they had even started their journey.

Wim looked reproachfully at Helene, and in the confusion of her emotions she began an elaborate search in her jacket pockets. For what, she knew not. Wim turned away from her, and thus rejected, she wandered across to join the others.

As Suzanne ran across to the bungalow she remembered an old wide-brimmed straw hat Wim had always kept for her on a hook behind the kitchen door. She found it, still where she had left it, and stuck it gleefully on to the back of her head to satisfy her mother.

She ran back to Wim. He looked up from what he was doing. "It still suits you," he said, approvingly.

Suzanne patted the hat and gave a sly glance towards her mother, who was now some distance away, talking to Claire.

Wim was ready to move off. He looked round at the party for which he would be responsible for the next week or so and calculated on their behaviour.

He had been taken unawares by the two extra guests but was quite good-natured about their coming along. Paul looked as if he might be useful. The girl Erica was a beauty. Such sad eyes, though. He noticed her loose-limbed elegance. She, too, was wearing a jacket and slacks, but in pale blue linen with an open necked long-sleeved white silk shirt. So comfortable, yet so suitable. Her chestnut hair was tied back, but there were close curls in the fine hair at her temples. All this was not lost on Wim.

As for Erica herself, she had been surprised by her reaction to Wim. She wondered how old he was and guessed he was round about forty. His attraction was at once obvious to her. It might be rather interesting to find out about him, a thought flickered, but died almost as soon as it was born. Her recent past was too painful. She turned to meet Claire and Vincent Landers.

"Hi, there!" said Claire, without formality.

Erica was intrigued by the sack of potatoes wearing a pith helmet advancing towards her, yet her smile was gracious. Erica's heart knew no unkindness. "Hi!" she replied.

Claire spread an infectious gaiety.

"When are you going to get a wife to share this lovely home with you?" She was calling to Wim as she leaned against the veranda rail, surveying him with amusement and fanning herself with a magazine she had picked up from one of the tables.

"Time enough for that, Claire," he called back good-humouredly.

"Well, you've had enough chances, heaven only knows."

For a second or two Wim paused, then he said, "True, true." But this time he didn't smile. Claire's matchmaking tactics were inclined to wear thin, and also somewhat embarrassing at times.

Against his will his eyes sought Helene, but he abruptly held out his hand to Suzanne. "Come, Suzy, I almost forgot. I have something to show you." He was irritated by Claire's remarks, even though he knew she meant no harm.

Erica watched as the two sauntered over towards the stables. She thought they made an attractive pair: both so blond, but Wim so bronzed it made him look the lighter of the two. Suzanne was smiling up at him, in her ridiculous hat, as if she owned him. "They are so alike they could be father and daughter," thought Erica, "How strange . . ."

"Well, Suzy," said Wim, when they were out of earshot, "You're looking very perky this morning."

"It's good to be home." She smiled sideways at him. "I'm glad you're better tempered today."

He threw back his head and laughed. Her remark banished his annoyance with Claire.

They walked on.

"Tell me about the girl Erica," he said.

"She and her brother came out on the same aircraft as I did."

"You made friends of them?"

"Not until they turned up at Tamarisk Bay. Erica was very uncommunicative on the journey out. She hardly opened her eyes. I thought she was ill."

"And was she?"

"She *has* been. Her brother told me she'd just come out of hospital."

"Is she fit enough to stand up to coming with us, d'you think?"

"Oh, yes, Wim, I'm sure she is."

"She had better be. We don't want any difficulties to arise when once we leave."

"No, I'm sure you won't have any trouble with her."

"Good." Then he abruptly changed the subject. They had arrived at the stables. "I've bought a new pony. Her name is

Sheena. Tell me what you think of her."
He went to the end stall. "Here she is."

Sheena was black and glossy. Suzanne
stroked the pony's nose. "She's quite big
for a pony." She undid the stall and led
Sheena out and walked her round. "She
seems to be very gentle. You don't usually
chose gentle ones. Who's she for?"

"I thought perhaps your mother. She
might like a quiet mount. It might
encourage her to ride more."

Suzanne was thoughtful. "She might."
She paused. Inwardly she doubted the
possibility. "What will you do with her if
she doesn't?"

"Ride her myself."

"Ha, ha. A quiet horse would never
satisfy *you*."

"Perhaps not. Anyway, it's a try. I
thought you'd like to see her. *You*, of
course, my girl, may ride her any time you
wish. You know that."

"Thanks, but what about Jason? He
might be jealous."

"Oh, well . . . you're welcome, anyway.
Perhaps you'll mention it to your mother."

"Why can't you?"

He shrugged. "I should prefer you to do it."

"All right. I'll tell her, if you like."

They walked back to join the others, Suzanne delighted to tell her mother of Wim's offer, but Helene appeared to make little response. Suzanne felt quite sorry that Wim might have gone to so much trouble for so little result.

Wim indicated that he was going to make a final check on arrangements. Suzanne sought out Erica.

"We must be quick, but would you like me to show you the bungalow before we go?"

Erica nodded.

Suzanne then proceeded to give Erica a tour of inspection as if the bungalow had been her own.

Erica had already seen the outside. It was built of stone and looked as if nothing could ever move it. It had been designed to nestle against the hillside and merge with the landscape, and the architect had succeeded in his undertaking.

As well as the front veranda, there was a second one on a higher level at the back of the building, which looked across to the mountains. This was even more spacious, and Erica loved the high ceiling. As she looked up she could see two small lizards darting about, but what they could find to eat she could not imagine, since the whole veranda was screened with pale green fine wire mesh so that no flying insects could penetrate.

Erica tapped it lightly with her long slender fingers.

"Oh, that!" said Suzanne. "It keeps the place free of mosquitoes . . . although *some* always manage to get in . . . lizards love them," she continued, pointing upwards. "Have you ever seen them move? They're like lightning. Watch."

Erica looked up.

The structure that held the screening was white-painted wood lattice. Flowering shrubs—scarlet poinsettia, pale blue plumbago, salmon pink oleander and brilliant orange hibiscus—surrounded the outside, making the inside a perfect arbour. Mauve and pale pink bougainvillaea trailed up the sides, and the front was kept clear for a view of the mountains.

For shade there were several Chinese elms, pruned and trained with care into umbrella shapes. Erica wondered if the resourceful Wim had tended them himself or whether an expert was called in at intervals.

Furniture with more flowered linen seat covers were worth a try . . . "Um, nice," Erica murmured. But Suzanne was impatient for her to see the remainder of the bungalow.

"This is the lounge." Suzanne opened the door to the cool, long room with its sturdy leather furniture. "Though Wim doesn't call it a lounge. He calls it the bar."

Erica glanced round the overly masculine room, and her eyes alighted on the bar across the corner and could see an ample store of liquor. Beyond was a dining-room, and beyond that a large modern well-equipped kitchen.

"Very comfortable," said Erica, feeling that some remark was obligatory.

Then Suzanne made for the bedroom which she knew her mother had helped Wim prepare for Merle. It was still a mystery to her why Merle had gone.

As her hand reached for the door knob she was wondering if the colours would have the same impact on Erica as they had on her the morning she went to say goodbye to Wim before she left for England. Her mother had come with her and they had all gone into the room to admire it.

Restful cool greens and blues merging to give a misty look. "It's like the sea and sky meeting," Suzanne remembered her mother saying. The gauzy drapes on the carved pale wood four-poster bed were the most glamorous mosquito nets she had ever seen. So well chosen were they she could never decide whether they were actually blue or green.

As she turned the handle she said to Erica, *"This* is *my* favourite room." She spoke in a hushed tone, almost reverently, as if about to show off a priceless gem.

But the door did not yield and she gasped with astonishment. "Oh!" she cried, "It's locked!" She turned to see Wim standing there behind them. He was angry.

Suzanne looked up at him, aghast— completely bewildered by the closed door.

Erica pretended to be polishing her

sunglasses. An acute embarrassment had overcome her. She realised at once that Suzanne had taken rather a liberty in showing her Wim's home without his permission.

"It's time we were going," he said, curtly.

Suzanne was mortified. Her cheeks were burning. The visit was quite spoilt for her. Wim should have warned her. He would have in the old days, she thought, when she came and went just as she pleased, treating the place as if it had been her own home.

They walked back through the bungalow in silence to where the others were waiting to depart.

Nothing had been forgotten. It seldom was if Wim was in command.

The convoy of vehicles moved off, Wim leading in his own six-seater station wagon, a comfortable vehicle which had been modified to his own specification, and allowed plenty of room for the equipment they were taking. Some of it was strapped to the roof.

Beside Wim sat Paul, rather over-awed by Wim's efficiency, and behind him, on the back seat, Erica. Helene and Suzanne travelled with Ben in his Pinto, and Claire and Vincent followed in their Range Rover.

Erica, sitting behind Wim, looked at his back as he handled the wheel on the bumpy road. His powerful muscles barely moved. She could see the blond hairs on his arm glistening in the sun on his tanned skin and felt an involuntary reaction as if she had experienced an intimacy.

As for Suzanne, she was endeavouring to recover from her rebuff: She was less than happy about being in the Pinto with her mother and Ben Johnson. She had been hoping to sit beside Wim. Now the memory of a locked room reminded her once again that her world had changed out of all recognition.

The ever unfolding panorama of mountains and sparkling sea shimmered in the mid-morning sun. It was already hot, but the breeze kept the temperature bearable in the open sided vehicles.

Erica had rested her arm on the window edge only to find that within five minutes her sensitive skin was burning. She rolled down her shirtsleeves and the breeze played inside them to keep her comfortable.

Wim's plan was to drive east from St. Louis and keep to the coast road the whole way round the island except for the northern tip. Here the mountains ran down into the sea in buttresses of rocky black lava, unchanged over thousands of years, ever since the volcano, "Keinou" as the islanders called it, had ceased to erupt.

The coast road was palm-shaded and ran for about twenty miles at the perimeter of a coconut plantation. Through the trees were glimpses of the sea and Wim suggested they might like to swim.

Erica was delighted at the prospect, but would have to watch that she didn't stay in too long. Her skin was by no means yet acclimatised to the tropical sun.

Three happy hours were spent on the long stretch of silver sand, and under the palms Wim and Claire organised a light snack and cold drinks.

The party carried on until an hour before sundown, when Wim decided they should make camp.

They had taken the road inland for a short distance, to a small lake that was surrounded by tamarisk and acacia trees where countless species of birds enjoyed an almost uninterrupted existence.

Wim, Ben and Paul erected the tents in a nearby clearing, and Claire, Suzanne and Erica got on with preparing the evening meal. Helene sat and watched in a brooding silence.

When the tents were up, Suzanne, Erica and Paul collected wood for the fire. Although they had brought plenty of charcoal for cooking, they liked to watch the leaping flames of a log fire. It gave them not only a sense of security, but one of comradeship.

"I think we'll build the fire to last the whole night," said Wim.

Out came folding canvas chairs and tables, and when they finally sat down to supper they were hungry. Baked ham spiked with cloves had been heated in a square iron oven resting on glowing charcoal. Also baked potatoes in their jackets and tinned peas and corn. Claire had peeled and sliced a large fresh pineapple to accompany the ham, and eight hungry people soon ate it all.

The evening sky glowed crimson as the party relaxed after their well-earned supper. As they sat there in the fleeting moments of dusk, a group of herons flew across the lake, silhouetted against the sunset. They looked quite rosy as they passed out of the sun's path. It was a perfect setting. One of those unbelievable moments of nature when every small incident falls exactly into place, just as the instruments in an orchestra combine, to make a perfect harmony. Unexpected and unforgettable.

Some time later Suzanne began to yawn, and then Claire. They decided to retire, followed by several others.

There were four tents. Helene, Erica and Suzanne took one, Ben and Paul shared the second, Claire and Vincent the third. Wim had the fourth to himself.

During the day, Wim had been very much aware of Helene's tenseness, and had reached a point where he was determined to speak to her alone, if only for five minutes. So when the others left the fire and reluctantly made their way to bed, he made a discreet sign for her to stay.

The others noticed nothing unusual in that Helene should linger, but Ben did. He felt something was going on. What it was he didn't know. But because he had taken Dr. Grayson's place on the trip he felt a certain responsibility towards Mrs. Grayson and Suzanne. He looked across at Mrs. Grayson. There were deep shadows under her eyes, even allowing for the fire-light. She looked pale. He said, innocently, "Mrs. Grayson, are you sure this journey isn't too strenuous for you?"

Helene was taken aback. Why on earth should he have said that? Why didn't he go to his tent? The others had departed long ago.

Now that Ben was showing concern, Wim realised it was going to be difficult to get Helene on his own without being conspicuous.

"You *do* look a bit peaky, Helene." He stood up. "I'll just make up the fire. We'll all turn in now." He made an effort to appear casual. And with that, he pulled a couple of large logs across on to the fire so that it would burn steadily until the early hours of the morning.

"Why do doctors always fuss?" Helene glared at Ben and went angrily across to her tent, where Suzanne and Erica appeared to be already asleep.

She was about to undress when she heard Wim's voice saying softly, "Helene . . ." She opened the flap to see him beckoning.

"Come for a walk," he whispered. "It's such a beautiful night."

When they were well away from the tents he said, "Ben's Pinto is missing. I wonder what he is playing at!"

"Who cares," said Helene. Her voice was melancholic.

Wim stopped in his tracks and put an arm round her. She buried her face against his shoulder.

He said, kindly, "Come over to my tent. I'll give you a brandy."

She reached up to put her arms around him. "You are always so good to me," she murmured, tears rushing to her eyes.

Erica was not asleep. She lay for some time listening to the small sounds of night and the intermittent wind that rustled the tops of the trees.

How right Paul had been to get her away from England. It was good for him, too. She wondered what would have become of her had Paul not come to her rescue as he did. Everything had worked out so well. The trip out, the stay at Tamarisk Bay, and now the good fortune to have been able to accept the Graysons' invitation to come on a trip into the mountains. It was like a dream it was such a beautiful island. And so unexpected. She had not known such an island or way of life existed. She had been so busy in her own world, working and working for success. It had finally come to her, but when it had there had been a man unscrupulous enough to use her personal success for his own ends. What a despicable thing he had done to her, and yet she blamed herself for letting it happen. Surely there must have been some way I could have known what he was really like . . . She inhaled deeply and turned in her bed. Never mind all that, she told herself, it's over. Finished. Dead. Her thoughts moved across to Suzanne, and then to Helene's empty bed. "I wonder why she *is* so unhappy," she thought. "She appears to have everything any woman could possibly want. An adoring husband and loving daughter, an exciting life and no money worries. If all those things cannot make her happy there must be something seriously wrong. She appears to be constantly frustrated, restless. . . yearning . . . yet how much would I give to be in her situation. She appears to have everything life can offer . . . even Wim. Wim? Yes, that must be it. She wants Wim . . ." But Erica felt herself slipping into sleep. Already her sympathies were outside of herself and she could again think of others.

6

BEN had driven away in the Pinto without telling anyone, but he wasn't entirely sure himself why he had done so. He was only certain of one thing: that Dr. Grayson should be alerted that his wife needed her husband with her.

He drove on and on through the night until at last he reached St. Louis. He made straight for the hospital as he guessed Dr. Grayson would still be there, working in his laboratory or perhaps sleeping for a few hours on the couch in his office.

Ben was cautious. He wanted to persuade the doctor to go and fetch his wife without alarming him in any way. As he surmised, he was at the hospital, but in his office seated at his desk.

"What on earth are you doing here?" was the doctor's reaction. "I should have thought you would all have been halfway up Keino by now."

"We were heading that way."

"Were?"

"I've come back to persuade you to join the others, sir."

"For what reason?"

"It's Mrs. Grayson."

"Is she ill? Tell me." Edmund was becoming agitated. "No, sir, she isn't ill. But she doesn't look too well. I feel the journey may be too much for her." He paused, unable to explain further.

The doctor said, "What do you think I should do?"

"It's up to you, Doctor. But could you possibly come back with me and see her for yourself?"

"But I cannot possibly leave the hospital. There is no one to take charge."

"In that case I had better stay." Ben was adamant.

"But I shall never find them. Where are they?"

"Camped about ten miles inland at the bird sanctuary—Lake Angel. They won't be leaving until the car gets back. They don't even know I've gone, anyhow."

Dr. Grayson removed his white coat and reluctantly put on his jacket. "Don't you think you are making a mountain out of an ant hill, young man?"

Ben avoided the doctor's eyes and went across to open the door to speed the departure. He was relieved to be excused from returning to camp, knowing he would have to face an irate Mrs. Grayson.

Edmund climbed disconsolately into his Mercedes, sick at the thought of the long night drive. He had had a long, tiring day and felt a constriction in his chest. He knew Helene would not thank him for interfering, but what else could he do but comply with the boy's assessment of the situation? Ben must surely have had a good reason for coming back so late at night.

Dawn was breaking when Edmund finally found them. He parked his car, and as he walked unsteadily towards the tents, Wim emerged to greet him with some surprise.

"It's young Ben's idea. He thinks my wife is not well. I thought it best to come and see for myself."

Wim led the way to the tent where Helene was sleeping. "She's alone," he whispered, "the others have gone for a swim."

Edmund lifted the flap and entered the

tent where his wife lay, sleepless even in the early morning.

"Edmund!" She was startled.

"Ben thought you weren't looking too well last night, so he came to tell me," he said, lamely.

Helene looked incredulous. "Do you mean to say he went all the way back to the hospital just to tell you that? How absolutely ridiculous. I am perfectly well."

Edmund moved Helene's clothes from the folding stool beside her bed and sat down. "My dear," he said, gently, "I really think this journey may be too much for you. How about coming back with me?"

Helene's anger rose. "How dare that boy take it into his own hands to fetch you all this way for nothing. Where is he? I'll soon tell him what I think of his meddling."

Edmund placed a restraining hand on his wife's arm. "He isn't here, Helene. He gave up the trip because he was worried about you."

"It's just too ridiculous."

She put on her robe angrily, pulling at the sash as she tied it tight, then left the tent for a shower, leaving Edmund sitting there, weary and worried. He felt exhausted from the night's journey and the pain in his chest was increasing in intensity. He put his hand in his pocket and took out the bottle of pills, taking two, in the hope that they would ease his discomfort.

Claire, meanwhile, had learned from Wim what had happened and put her head round the tent flap. "Is there anything *I* can do?"

"Yes, there is, Claire," he replied, gratefully. "I know this is going to be difficult, but could you try and persuade her to come back with me?"

"Can't you ask her yourself?"

"I'd be grateful if *you* would do it."

Claire whistled. "I don't know, Ed. She'll be as mad as hell. You know that."

He nodded. "I feel too whacked to fight with her. I've been travelling all night."

"You poor dear. Wait . . . let's all have some breakfast together and I'll see what I can do, eh?"

He had to be satisfied with that. "I'll be out directly. Tell Wim we are going to persuade her to return with me. But I'll leave it to you to tell her. Please?"

"OK."

"Thanks."

Breakfast was not a happy occasion.

Wim adopted his non-committal attitude. Suzanne was puzzled. Erica and Paul noticed little except that one member of the party had disappeared while another had arrived. For all they knew this was the usual pattern, except . . . for some reason or other Claire was unusually quiet, and towards the end of the meal they sensed that something was amiss.

Helene looked pale. Edmund could eat nothing. He was too weary and upset. All he had was a cup of strong coffee. Helene toyed with her food and finally left it uneaten and disappeared into her tent.

Claire followed her.

"Calm down, honey."

"Calm down!" She felt like exploding. "How *can* I? I am *so* angry. He frustrates me in everything I ever want to do."

Claire waited some moments, then said, "You know you'll have to go back with him, don't you?"

"I absolutely refuse."

"Please see reason, Helene. You're not yourself. You're all tied up in knots. Be sensible. Go back."

Helene said, "I will not!" But she was busy gathering her things together and throwing them furiously into her case. "Anyhow, everything is spoilt, now."

"That's a good girl," said Claire, ignoring the last comment in her relief.

They walked across to the Mercedes. Helene got into the passenger seat and sat staring straight before her. She didn't even say goodbye to the others. She hated being dragged away. She turned to Claire as unshed tears of rage filled her eyes. "Will you explain to Wim for me?" Her lips quivered.

"Of course."

Edmund slowly made his way to the car. As he passed Claire she winked at him. He climbed into the driving-seat and the two moved off unhappily, not a word being spoken for the first ten miles.

Helene was still seething, and at last she blurted out, "I wish I had never come to this horrible island. I loathe it. I hate everything about it. I hate you, too . . .

the way you never spend any time with me . . . just leave me to manage my life the best way I can . . . and then, when I try to enjoy myself a little you manage to spoil it all. You know very well how much I've been looking forward to this trip . . . and what happens! That stupid young man decides I look a bit pale and out you trot to collect me as if I were a parcel. Making me look a stupid, helpless creature. . . which I most certainly am NOT."

Edmund said nothing. All he could feel was intense pain that his wife was so distraught. He was unable to separate the pain of her unhappiness from the pain in his chest.

Helene eventually turned to him and said, "Why don't you speak? Do you *have* to sit there looking like a martyr?"

"I have rather bad indigestion. Could you get that bottle out of my pocket and tip me out one of the pills?"

Helene was taken aback. She had not expected such a reply. Something warned her to take him seriously, and so she did as she was asked. She looked at the bottle. "These aren't indigestion tablets."

"They'll do . . . they are all I have with me."

"You should have had something to eat. That cup of coffee must have upset you," she said crossly. "When did you last eat?"

"I can't remember . . . yesterday breakfast, probably." Edmund was beginning to feel sorry for himself.

"And now you wonder why you have indigestion!" She spoke impatiently, as if he were a dolt. *"Really!"*

Edmund was waiting for the pill to relieve his pain. He hoped to spare his wife the truth.

She was gentler now. "Is it a little better?"

He nodded.

Helene turned to search the back seat and discovered a basket with a flask of tea and some rolls with cheese. Also some fruit. Wim must have put it there before he came to breakfast. Emotion welled up within her, realising that Wim had known what would be the outcome of Edmund's arrival. But also with gratitude that he had been so thoughtful. His constant care humbled her.

"Look," she said, "they've put us a

flask and something to eat. Let's stop for a while."

By the time they had eaten together and shared the flask of tea, they felt better. Helene's anger had now changed to concern for Edmund.

They had been sitting in the back of the car for their interlude, and when she sensed it was time to move on, she said, "Let *me* drive for a while." She got out and moved into the driving-seat.

"I'd forgotten how well you drive," said Edmund, grateful for the respite from driving, but mostly from her anger.

As Helene drove, her thoughts went back to what had first drawn her to Edmund. They were so very different— perhaps that had been it. He had been that much older and so much more placid than she was. But though well aware of her own need for his moral strength, she still felt he had no understanding of her own nature and needs. She, in turn, was unable to look at life from *his* point of view. All she could see was her own, and apparently Edmund was the same. She tried desperately to understand what he gained from helping others to the exclusion of herself, but remained unconvinced that she should come second to his vocation. When a life at the hospital had been saved and she saw the light of achievement in his eyes, all she could feel was jealousy at the unending line of patients who demanded his strength more and more and left so little of him for herself. Perhaps it would have been better if he had stayed single, since he was so dedicated to his work. Then she thought of Suzanne. Even Suzanne had been no particular bond between them. She thanked God he had never known the truth.

All the same, he had spent little of his time with her when she was tiny. It was Wim, always Wim, who took interest in her and showed her games to play. Wim's father had loved Suzanne, too. He had been dead five years now. What a wonderful man he had been, and so tough. He would work from dawn to dusk, even though he was well over seventy, and think nothing of it. Wim was going to be just the same. But Edmund . . . she must keep her thoughts on Edmund . . . sitting here beside her and for once needing her.

When they had first been married there had been the odd occasion when she had been able to comfort him when things were not going well at the hospital, but that didn't last very long. Gradually over the years he had confided in her less and less. And although she knew the fault was hers, she seemed incapable of putting things right.

"I have become intolerant and selfish with him," she groaned, inwardly. "How I wish I had never married him. My life would have been so different . . . and yet . . . if I had never come to Balandra I should never have met Wim . . . and perhaps . . . who knows? God, who does know? What *is* love all about?"

She turned to look at her husband. He was asleep.

Helene returned to concentrating on the road, and drove the whole way back to St. Louis, bypassing the hospital.

7

CLAIRE was sitting on a fallen tree, examining a sore toe where her shoes pinched. She was thinking about Helene and what she would tell Suzanne, who was at that moment coming towards her.

"Have you a spare Band-aid, Suzy, love? My toe is mighty sore."

"Yes, of course. Unless Mother has made off with them. I can't understand why she suddenly disappeared like that."

"She's not feeling too good, honey. Nothing much. It's just that this rough life doesn't suit her too well."

"She was keen enough to come."

"Yes, well, I expect she didn't realise what she was in for." Claire mustered a reassuring smile. "Get me a Band-aid, Suzy, there's a love," she repeated.

Suzanne walked away. Not in the direction of her own tent, but to Wim's. He must have been watching them, for he handed Suzanne a tin of sticking plasters before she even asked. He was afraid she was going to question him about her mother.

His awareness of Helene's emotional difficulties made him realise just how powerless he was to help her. She was frustrated beyond endurance, and most of it her own making. Wim's thoughts turned on her tenderness towards himself and her desperate need for a loving relationship.

Although at first he had taken it for granted that their young affair was basically a mutual sexual need that was bound to pass, he now realised it was not so. He loved her as he had loved no other woman, and it had lasted for twenty years.

But their relationship had got to the point when he was becoming dissatisfied. Either Helene should leave Edmund and marry him, or he would have to end it. The time had come when he wanted a wife to share his life in the accepted way. As for Helene, he knew that she desperately needed his love. But it was a selfish love in that she was not prepared to make sacrifices for him.

He wondered about her physical relationship with her husband. He could only assume it was less than satisfactory: she would certainly never discuss it with him. Somehow she had been shut out from her husband's life and Wim could only speculate that the reason for it was Edmund's commitment to the hospital which was tantamount to obsession.

His own close association with Helene had precluded his marriage with Merle. She would have been a good wife to him, he knew, even though the enthusiasm had been mostly on her side. It was only when she discovered how possessive Helene was that she knew it would be hopeless.

Helene had even had the temerity to insist on supervising the decoration and furnishing of the bedroom in Wim's bungalow which was to have been Merle's. Merle had finally given up and returned to Martinique a bitterly disappointed girl.

And now he found how much he was drawn to the girl called Erica. She had a captivating benevolence of spirit about her, even though he found her reserve baffling. He had tried time and time again to engage her in conversation, but she always shied away from anything more than generalities. She would not even meet his eyes. She would turn away or find some other excuse to avoid his gaze. It puzzled him.

Suzanne and Paul were some way away from the others. Paul had managed to steer Suzanne in the direction of the station wagon while they were waiting for the foursome to come to a decision. He caught her hand. It fluttered a little and was carefully withdrawn. She was experiencing a rising sense of irritation and flushed. She looked away and shaded her eyes with her hand to glance hopefully at the main party.

Paul presumed she was shy. "What are your plans for the future?" He made an effort to sound casual.

"I haven't any." Her answer was sharp.

There was a silence.

Relenting a little, she said, "I'm not quite sure, yet."

"What would you like to do?"

"I'd like people to stop pestering me about the future and let me enjoy the present." She looked straight at him. "It looks very much as if my mother is trying to sidetrack me into the family perfume business."

"Does that upset you?"

"Of course it does. I want to stay here on Balandra." She looked bleakly into the distance. "She never gives up." A bitterness crept into her voice. "I'll tell you one thing, though. I'm not leaving Balandra again, if I can help it. I've already been away from it far too long. I can't bear to even think about such a thing." She walked away from him, across to where the others were poring over the maps, laughing and arguing as to what direction they should take. If they had been honest with themselves they would have realised they were relieved that Helene had departed. Her presence had created an indefinable tension.

Wim looked around. The tents had all been taken down and everything stowed in the truck once again. He called, "Are you all ready to move off?" He then went across to Erica and held out his hand to her, saying, "Would you care to sit in front with me today?"

She looked at him thoughtfully, then accepted with a smile and climbed into the station wagon beside him.

Suzanne was annoyed. She herself had

counted on being with either Wim or Erica. The thought of sitting behind with Paul didn't please her. She would have to put up with his banter and it was beginning to pall. It wouldn't have been so bad if she had known how to counter his sophisticated repartee, but it was boring to be on the receiving end all the time.

It was early afternoon and Helene was sitting at her mahogany desk. For two hours she had been trying to write to her mother—to make some contact with her family in France. It was the only thing that came to mind which might help her.

In all the years she had lived on Balandra she had only been back to France once, and that was ten years ago. Yet she had corresponded regularly, and her mother, though engrossed in the family business, had always borne in mind that Helene felt she was in exile, always longing for France.

The waste-basket beside her desk was half full of rejections and the page before her held only the words, "Maman . . . I long to be with you . . ." It was as far as she could get before her thoughts began to whirl again. "It is hopeless," she said aloud to herself. "It is just no good. I *cannot* say what I want."

The sound of a vehicle arriving surprised her. Edmund was not expected for hours.

"Mon Dieu!" she reacted. *"Qu'est-ce-qui se passe?"*

It was Ben Johnson.

Ever since he had impulsively driven back from the mountains to fetch Dr. Grayson, Ben had suffered from an oppressive feeling that Mrs. Grayson was angry with him for interfering in her affairs. He now realised that he had been over-zealous in his action, but at the time it had seemed the right thing to do. He felt a compulsion to come and apologise. In view of his attraction to Suzanne, Mrs. Grayson was the last person he wanted to offend.

He straightened his already straight tie, squared his already square shoulders and walked smartly up the steps.

Helene came towards him, pen in hand. Her questioning gaze left him silent until she came to his rescue. His contrite expression left her in no doubt as to the reason for his visit.

"Well?" she said, half in remembered pique.

"I've come to . . ."

"Well, go on."

"I . . . that is . . ." he stopped.

She waited.

"Mrs. Grayson, are you still angry with me?"

Helene put the top on her fountain pen and laid it down on the nearby table. "No, not now," she said, slowly, remembering her painful disappointment, "but I *was*. Very angry. Whatever made you do it?" She indicated a chair and they both sat down.

"I just don't know *what* made me do it. I had some vague feeling that you were suffering unwelcome attentions . . . that you were upset. Not feeling well . . . or something . . ." he ended, lamely.

Helene stood up. "Would you like something cool to drink?"

"Something cold? Yes, please."

Helene went to find Adele, but changed her mind and opened the refrigerator herself. She took out a container of fresh grapefruit juice and poured it into a crystal jug, adding a dozen or so ice cubes. She placed it on a silver tray with two crystal glasses and carried it through to the veranda, where Ben was waiting. He half rose to take the tray from her, but she declined his offer with a movement of her head.

"Tell me, Ben," Helene began, "what is it that keeps my husband at the hospital so much?"

"I'm not sure what you mean, Mrs. Grayson."

"I mean just what I say. What keeps him so long at the hospital? He is *always* there. I hardly ever see him."

Ben toyed with his glass. "He loves his work, Mrs. Grayson. He really does. I don't think he realises how quickly the time passes."

"I see."

There was another silence. Ben was very anxious not to antagonise her again. "Mrs. Grayson, I should very much like to see what I can of Suzanne, if she is willing. Have you any objections?"

"Not in the least. But you know, don't you, that she won't be here for very long."

"Is she going away, then?"

"As soon as we have decided on her future. Yes."

Ben was crestfallen. He wondered if Suzanne knew of this. Probably not. She wouldn't be very pleased if she did. He decided to change the subject. "May I ask when they are all expected back?"

"I really don't know." Helene herself was anxious. "Perhaps today. Perhaps tomorrow."

"May I call in tomorrow evening?"

"If you wish."

Ben stood up. He was not convinced that Mrs. Grayson had forgiven him, but felt he had done what he could to make amends. He would have to wait and see.

Helene was not in the least concerned about Ben's feelings. She was too wrapped up in her own problems.

"Goodbye, Mrs. Grayson. I will call in tomorrow, then."

As he left, she picked up her pen again and walked back to her desk.

8

THE party had reached four thousand feet and could see the extinct volcano towering high above them. Their journey had so far taken them through the rain forest that covered the slopes now below them to the south.

Erica and Paul had suffered a sense of uneasy foreboding in this new strange world of oppressive humidity. The hot, odorous plant-life seemed to creep around them with a sinister strangulatory effect, vaguely threatening, so that by the time the sunlight had once more begun to penetrate the tall trees and the dense vegetation to thin out they experienced a deep relief. Yet, when once it was well behind them, Erica was so caught by its utter fascination that she was already poised in anticipation for the return journey.

To the north and west, green undulating hills rose in natural terraces where back in time immemorial intermittent lava flows had been emitted from above, and over the years carpeted with plant life.

Wim pulled into the side of the track and the others pulled up behind him. They got out of their vehicles and stood in silence. All they could hear was the soft sigh of the wind that flicked at them playfully.

Presently, Claire, looking as tumbled as an eiderdown, took off her pith helmet and pitched it into the back of their Range Rover. "I really can't think what made me bring it," she laughed, and turned to dislodge a giant-sized flask from her collection of accoutrements. Some drinking-glasses also appeared, and she smilingly served each member of the party with a rum punch.

"There," she said, victoriously, "that surprised you all, didn't it!"

Yes, it had, they were bound to admit it.

Suzanne had recovered her good spirits and now felt amiable towards Paul. It had been somewhat of an effort, but she had managed it.

It had been a revelation to her that she had enjoyed herself more because her mother was absent, but her own attitude towards Paul she found puzzling. Though her shyness had at last worn off and they had become better friends, she was still wary. What she could not quite understand, however, was why, whenever he approached her in any way, her defences sprang up. Even so, only that, morning as they had half waded, half climbed the rocks at the foot of some falls, Paul had held her hand to prevent her from slipping. She felt no antogonism then. They had both looked up at the cascading heights together to see the rainbow that spanned the gorge. It was like discovering a secret . . . and yet it was Wim who pointed out that the rainbow was always there when the sun shone.

They had then climbed the hill overlooking the falls and had walked through groves of heavily scented frangipani. Suzanne recalled how she had tactfully tried to disengage Paul's hand by walking round a gnarled flamboyant tree now shedding its fiery blossoms to form a carpet on the brown-red earth.

Suddenly Paul was beside her again.

"When the time comes for me to leave I am going to hate it," he said, quietly.

Suzanne turned to him. "Must you go?"

"Of course. I must get back to my business—or there won't be any business to get back to."

"And Erica, too? Oh dear, we shall miss you both."

"Will you Suzy?" It was the first time he had called her that.

She bit her lip. Without thinking she had inadvertently encouraged him.

Paul put his arm around her shoulders, making it as casual a gesture as he could. But Suzanne had to brace herself not to pull away from him.

It had taken them four days to get to the crater, and up in the rarefied atmosphere it was so cool they needed to put on warmer clothing.

They would have to walk the last mile. The track had petered out long since, but they had kept going by choosing fairly smooth ground and making a gradual ascent between boulders. Now they found their progress was blocked by hardened shoulders of black lava too close together for access. Somewhat forbidding, the land-scape was softened considerably by the profusion of ferns and grasses that had found a foothold in the crevices.

Wim checked his fuel and was satisfied they had enough for the return journey despite the climb having been rather more extravagant on fuel than he had bargained for. They would need to go carefully when it came to the descent.

But this afternoon they would pitch the tents, have an evening meal and contem-plate on the walk up to the crater early next morning.

Claire was relieved that the day's travel-ling was over. The high altitude made her feel tired, but Vincent was wiry and ready for anything.

After supper, Wim sought out Erica and engaged her in general conversation. Suzanne was piqued. She eyed them for some time until Paul noticed her and suggested they went for a walk.

Suzanne made a gesture of annoyance, but went with him.

This time, Paul didn't attempt to be facetious but managed to get her interested in talking about Wim's plantation, which she was only too pleased to do.

When they returned, they joined Erica and Wim, who were still sitting beside the fire. Claire and Vincent were clearing the remains of supper and engaging in a duet which ended in laughter when Vincent's voice ended in a croak.

Suzanne was still piqued that Wim's attention should have turned to Erica, so that as the two of them sat down, she said, casually, "Isn't it a shame that Paul and Erica have to go back soon."

Wim immediately expressed surprise. "Go back! Where?"

"England, of course. Where do you suppose?"

"I hadn't realised they were only on holiday."

"Why yes," cut in Paul, "I must get back to my needle and thread."

"Are you a tailor, then?" asked Wim.

Paul laughed. "I'm in what is lightly called 'the rag trade'."

"Must Erica go, too?" exclaimed Suzanne.

"Well, yes. That is, unless she wants to stay on for a while. Do you, Sis?"

"I don't know," she replied, quietly, "but I'd like to think about it."

"What's this I hear?" Claire was alert. She walked over to join them. "Erica leaving us? Oh no, honey, please don't. Stay on with us for a bit. Vin and I would love to have you stay with us. Please."

"That's very kind of you, Claire. Are you sure you have room for me?"

"I should imagine so. We have six bedrooms, and Vin and I only use one at a time." She smiled. "We've been waiting for the chance to ask you. We thought of it weeks ago, didn't we, Vin?"

Vincent nodded. "We certainly did."

They must all have taken it for granted that Erica could do as she pleased. She was relieved that no one questioned her.

A morning mist covered the crater at dawn, but the six set out in anticipation that it would lift as the sun rose higher. They weren't disappointed. It rose like a veil as they traversed the last hundred yards of steep rocky lava to a fissure where once the molten flow had made its final bid.

Wim led the way, and they picked their

footsteps carefully over grass-grown spatter cones until all at once they were looking into a crater half a mile across and so deep it looked unfathomable.

As they peered down into the green Garden of Eden they could not help but be affected by its beauty. The climb had been hard, but the sight that met them was every bit worth the effort.

Keino had ceased its eruption roughly ten thousand years ago. The exterior shield profile of the volcano had remained unaltered, even though the interior was a gutted shell. Yet within that shell the moisture-laden trade winds had brought so much rain that it nurtured the vegetation clinging to the almost vertical sides. Birds and butterflies had found refuge there, sheltered as they were, on all sides.

With little difficulty the six discovered that it was possible to walk around the caldera on the inside. It took them an unhurried two hours.

They left Keino the following morning, but Wim knew that the volcano had not been the high point of the journey. That was yet to come.

When the tents were dismantled and everything stowed away, they got back into the vehicles and he led the way slowly down the mountainside until he reached the point where they had first left the track. He now turned south and then west, following the curve of the mountain they had left.

Now the terrain was changing to lush green water-carved buttresses and they saw waterfalls cascading from crevices high up. Soon they rounded a particularly difficult bend to come upon a breathtakingly beautiful lapis lazuli lake which seemed to go on for ever in a colossal amphitheatre.

No one spoke.

Wim turned to Erica and smiled at her as she sat beside him and she felt a rush of emotion as she fought against tears at the sight of such beauty.

They skirted the lake for a couple of miles or so then Wim saw a suitable stopping-place. They would camp here for two or three days before making the journey back to St. Louis.

Erica made her way to the edge of the dazzling expanse of blue with its backdrop of mountains and volcano, aware that Wim was following her.

They were now quite some distance from the others.

Erica stopped, conscious now that Wim was regarding her steadily. She turned to him in response, but he looked away, shading his eyes with his hand . . . thoughtful, remote.

Erica was puzzled, until her uncanny intuition told her that no doubt Wim had his own difficulties. He had followed her, and knowing this, she sensed his need. She had already noticed the possessive element in his friendship with the Graysons. Both Helene and Suzanne appeared to regard him as their own special property. A shaft of compassion for him caught her unawares, but outwardly she remained as serene as the blue lake.

Wim glanced at her again, there beside him, so still. He likened her to a frangipani blossom—so deep and scented and beautiful—and yet so vulnerable. He would, perhaps, be afraid to touch her petals in case she might bruise too easily. Perhaps such tenderness as she asked for might not be within his power.

Then suddenly Helene was standing beside him—just as surely as if in reality —and an intense disquiet filled him, sending shivers down his spine.

There had been so much love between them that had never been expressed. A smouldering volcano that went on and on, tormenting them both with its fury. If only she had left Edmund . . . but try as he might he had never been able to persuade her to do so. It was difficult to understand why she was so adamant. He frowned . . . and now their love had turned to despair. He sometimes wondered how he could go on: he needed a wife. Someone who would completely belong to him and share his life.

Erica, still silent, calmed him. Somehow she interpreted his mood. Unaccountably, he took her hand, kissed it lightly and released it, then folded his arms and stared across the lake.

Erica put the same hand on his shoulder with a gentle pressure, then she turned and walked back to the others, leaving him standing there.

They spent the next three days beside

the lake, and though Erica extended companionship to Wim, she was careful never again to place him in an emotional situation. Never ever would she want to come between Helene and Wim: their relationship was obviously a very complex one. But she enjoyed his company to the full and decided to let fate handle her own situation.

Back at Wim's bungalow the sorting out was done and they all sat down for a rum punch together before going their separate ways.

Suzanne went into the kitchen and returned the faded straw hat to its hook. It was more squashed than when she took it. She had sat on it more than she had worn it. "At least I haven't lost it yet," she thought. "It looks better on the kitchen door anyway. Part of me still belongs here." She was still trying to convince herself.

Wim walked across to Vincent's Range Rover with Erica and Paul. He looked into Erica's eyes and said, "Get Claire to bring you and Paul over. I'll show you around the plantation."

Erica smiled at him. "We'd love to come."

"I shall be very busy for two or three days, but shall be clear by the weekend. How about Sunday?"

Claire leaned out of the passenger window. "Does that include us?" She was laughing.

"No, but I suppose I shall have to put up with you, since you'll be driving them over." He grinned. "Come to lunch."

Claire laughed as the Range Rover moved off.

Erica turned. Wim was standing with hands on hips, watching them depart. She waved until they were out of sight.

Wim took Suzanne home, but pulled up outside the picket gate, well away from the house.

"Aren't you coming in?"

"No, Suzy. I must get back. There's a lot to do as I've been away."

"Before you go I want to ask you something."

"Well?"

"You like Erica, don't you?"

"Yes, I do, very much."

"So do I." She was very quiet, not attempting to get out of the station wagon.

"Is there something you want to tell me, Suzanne?"

"Yes, but I can't."

"Why not?"

"I don't know . . . oh dear . . . I'd so like to say, but I can't."

He waited patiently. "What's it all about?"

But she shook her head and looked down at her hands. Wim let the moment pass, just as he had with Erica. But he said, quietly, "Have *you* enjoyed the past few days, Suzy?"

"Oh, yes. It's been marvellous. Thank you."

She impulsively kissed his cheek as she had done so often as a child. But as she opened the door and jumped down from the vehicle she felt vexed that she had. Glancing up at him quickly as he leaned towards her she looked into his eyes, trying desperately to find herself in them, but could not.

She slammed the station wagon door, saying, "I really believe I'm too old to kiss you now . . ." and laughed awkwardly.

Then she ran across the paddock and into the house, and when she reached her unfamiliar bedroom she flung herself on her bed and wept for her childhood.

9

DURING the next few weeks, Suzanne's pleasure at being home again was marred by her resentment towards her mother.

She had no special reason to justify herself. It was just an insidious feeling of coldness towards her. There was no direct evidence of the reason for it, yet a cold, unseen hand seemed to clutch at her heart when she thought of her own relationship with Wim. And as time passed, she experienced an irritability that was foreign to her nature. She found herself inwardly criticising everything her mother did and said. Not the least of it was her mother's apparent disregard for her father. She was indignant that his obvious tiredness seemed to be ignored. He spent most of his evenings at the hospital and rarely went out socially.

"Don't you ever worry about Father looking so tired?" Suzanne asked her mother, coldly.

Helene shrugged her shoulders. "I did once upon a time. But no longer. Whatever I said to him would make no difference. Your papa's work is his first love. I have had to make a life of my own or be bored to death."

Suzanne did not reply. How could her mother be so unfeeling, she wondered.

Helene changed the subject. "At least he has consented to come to the theatre tonight."

"Does that include me?"

"Of course. We have asked Paul and Erica, as well."

Why does Mother never tell me anything until it is all settled, she wondered. She could at least have mentioned it.

"Wear the coffee guipure tonight, Suzanne." Helene was at her most positive.

"I'd rather not, Mother, if you don't mind. I'd like to wear my new dress with the shirring."

"Nonsense! That is entirely unsuitable —only fit for the beach. Why, it does not even have shoulder straps."

"I don't think that matters. It's so

comfortable, and . . . anyway, I feel good in it."

"And since when has comfort anything to do with style?"

"I . . ."

"Oh, well," said Helene impatiently, "if you must make yourself look ridiculous, go ahead. I shall not stop you."

"Mother," pleaded Suzanne, "I *do* wish you wouldn't keep trying to make me wear those clothes you sent to Paris for. I'm so unhappy in that sort of thing."

"I suppose you are going to turn out to be one of those hopeless women who have absolutely no dress sense whatever, and no inclination to do anything about it."

"I love the way Erica dresses. Why can't I be like her?"

"You are not in the least like Erica. To begin with, you would look ridiculous in a caftan, but on Erica it is perfect."

Suzanne kept quiet. She was not convinced that her mother was correct. After all, she was tall and slim like Erica. So why not! But the knowledge didn't make her any keener to dress the way her mother wanted her to. She would say no more, but made up her mind that if her mother tried to force her to wear the lace dress that evening she would refuse to go. She was sure her father would back her up if it came to the point.

But for once he didn't. He came home early, still very tired, and Helene wasted no time in confronting him with Suzanne's attitude. He felt disinclined for a scene with his wife and so he sided with her. But Suzanne, disappointed as she was that her father had let her down, stood her ground.

"Either I wear what *I* like, Father, or I don't come. I really don't mind one way or another."

Edmund was astounded. He looked up at her, sternly.

"Do as your mother wishes, Suzanne."

"No." She hesitated. "It's about time I was allowed to wear just what I like, and I intend to, from now on."

The whole thing is getting out of hand, thought Edmund, wearily.

"Please, chérie." Her mother was cajoling now.

"No," said Suzanne. "I'm sorry, but no."

Helene was furious.

And so Suzanne put on her new dress.

Placing a fluffy white mohair stole around her shoulders, she smiled at her reflection in the mirror, and as she left her bedroom to join her parents, who were already waiting in the car, she felt quite two inches taller.

Suzanne was in her bedroom. Her mother didn't seem inclined to talk to her and her father had come home looking so weary again she felt it would be a good idea to keep out of his way.

She was idly turning the pages of a magazine when there was a tap on her door.

"Erica! How lovely to see you."

Erica smiled. "Well, we had to come over because Paul is going home tomorrow and he wants to say goodbye."

"Already?"

"I'm afraid so." She hesitated. "Suzanne . . . he's waiting on the veranda. I think he wants to talk to you. Could you spare him a few moments?"

Suzanne's heart gave a lurch. "Oh, no," she thought, "not *that* again." But she said, "Of course. Where is he, did you say? On the veranda?"

They walked through to the living-room and Erica sat down with the others. Suzanne reluctantly went through to where Paul was waiting. She walked slowly towards him.

"Suzy," he said, when they had walked round to the other side of the house, "I've come to say cheerio."

Suzanne said, lamely, "I'm sorry you're going so soon."

"Are you really, Suzy?" He gave a one-sided smile. "I wish I could believe that."

"Yes, of course I'm sorry. We all are . . . we've all had such a good time together."

"I was hoping I meant just a little more than that to you." He sought her hand. "Don't I?"

She hardly knew what to say. Paul waited in vain. There was a long silence between them. Finally, he said, "Your mother tells me you'll soon be going back to France."

"I'm *what!* It's the first I've heard of it." Her eyes flashed angrily.

"I'm sorry. I thought you knew all about it."

"Well, I *don't!*" She almost turned and

ran to accuse her mother in front of the others, but managed to control her feelings. She felt the blood rushing to her face.

"Please, Suzy. If or when you do come to Europe—*may* I see you? I couldn't leave without asking this."

Suzanne was silent, inwardly seething at her mother's arbitrary attitude in planning her future without even consulting her.

"Please write to me, at least," he begged.

She nodded, unsmiling, then slowly turned and walked back towards the lounge, with Paul following her disconsolately.

"Tell me, Paul," said Helene, noting his discouraged air, "How can we get in touch with you?"

"I've written everything down. Here." He abstractedly handed Helene a slip of paper and she walked across to put it underneath the glass paperweight on her desk.

"Well," said Claire, breaking into the silence, "suppose we'd better shuffle off." She turned to Edmund. "Are you OK, Ed? You look very tired."

Dr. Grayson stood up. "I'm fine, Claire. I've just had a busy day, that's all."

When the others had left, Suzanne said fiercely, "What did Paul mean, Mother, when he said he understood I was going back to France?"

Edmund intervened. "What's that?"

Suzanne turned to him. "Paul seems under the impression that I'm being sent to France." She was shaking with anger.

They both stared at Helene.

"Well," she said, defiantly, "if you must know—he's interested in Suzanne and I told him I expected she would be going to France soon, so that he'd have an opportunity of seeing her again."

"Where and what would Suzanne be doing there, may I ask?"

"At the château, I suppose. She ought to go into the family business—if she has any sense at all."

"*What?*" said Suzanne, horrified. "*Mother*, how *could* you!"

Edmund said, "I'll talk to you later, Suzanne." To his wife, he said, "Let's understand this, Helene. When there is a decision to be made regarding anyone in this family I want to be consulted. Do you understand?"

Helene blanched. She rose from her chair and went to her bedroom without saying a word. She was unused to being rebuked. Edmund had never spoken to her in such a tone before. She could hardly believe it.

After Helene had gone out of the room, Edmund said, "Have you any views of your own as to what you would like to do?"

"Yes, Father, I have."

"You want to stay here on the island?"

"Of course. It's my home."

Edmund picked up his pipe and filled it, but said nothing.

"Can't I have just a few months to myself? Is that *too* much to ask?"

"Of course you may." He paused. "Whoever told you otherwise?"

"Then I may have a holiday until after Christmas?"

"Certainly." He lighted his pipe, then said, "Don't you think it would be a kind gesture to go with the others tomorrow when they see Paul away? Because you have disappointed him there is no reason for treating him unkindly."

"But I haven't treated him unkindly. I've been very nice to him. Perhaps that's something else you haven't realised. . . with Mother's encouragement he has, in my own opinion, *forced* his attentions on me. Paul is a pleasant young man, but I have absolutely no intention of furthering the relationship."

"And that's all you have to say?"

"Yes, Father. I don't want to go to see him off tomorrow, and I don't *intend* to. I'm sorry, but there it is."

Dr. Grayson merely glanced at her, then picking up his book, commenced reading.

The following day, when Suzanne returned from an early morning ride, she found her mother still in bed with her breakfast tray untouched.

"Are you feeling ill, Mother?"

Helene sat up carefully. She felt dizzy, but managed to reply. "No, not ill. . . but not too good. I shall be all right presently. Hand me my shawl please, *chérie*."

Suzanne picked up the cream fringed silk shawl and gently draped it around her mother's shoulders. Helene was touched by the tenderness and two large tears escaped.

Suzanne's compassion was aroused and she forgot their differences for the moment. "I'm so sorry. Is there anything I can do?"

Helene shook her head and searched for her handkerchief without success.

"Let me get you a tissue. Here?" She opened the dressing-table drawer as her mother indicated. "Shall I pull the curtains back?"

"No. The light hurts my eyes." She dabbed at them carefully, trying to stem the tears, but they kept coming.

Suzanne was at a loss to know what to say or do. She was now used to her mother's rapid changes of mood, but unable to decide what was wrong.

"Leave me, *chérie*. I am better left alone. I'll get up later."

Suzanne kissed her gently and tried to arrange the bedclothes and pillows as her mother liked them. "See you later then." She smiled sympathetically and withdrew. Forgiveness, then, came easily to Suzanne.

She felt she really ought to tell her

father. Perhaps she would do so if her mother didn't improve as the day wore on.

It was midnight. Edmund was reluctant to leave his chair on the veranda. Tonight his book had remained unopened. He had much to think over and needed to clear his mind of any regrets for the decision he had made that morning.

It was strange that almost as soon as he had come to terms with that decision, Suzanne had rung him to say that Helene was still unwell. "It isn't that she's sick or anything," she had said, "but she keeps crying all the time."

"Don't worry, Suzanne. I'll be home as soon as I can. I have been half expecting this. Just be kind to her."

He put down the telephone and went to find Ben Johnson.

No longer could he ignore the fact that his wife was past the point of no return with her unsettled behaviour and disrupting influence so far as his work was concerned. It had become impossible for him to concentrate on his duties, let alone the research he was so anxious to continue.

There was so much to be done at the hospital.

He had no worries concerning handing over to his deputy—Ben Johnson was an excellent choice. It was just the disheartening feeling of not being able to give as much of himself as he would like, and the pressures within him had built up so much that it was affecting him physically as well as mentally.

He considered his age. At forty-eight he should not be so tired all the time. Helene had spoken of it. He wondered whether their lack of intimacy had given her this absurd notion that he no longer cared for her, always putting his job first.

"What *can* a man do? He *has* to put his job first. She seems to think her own wishes are paramount. Lately she has been almost impossible with her rapid changes of mood. Sometimes downright antagonistic towards me . . . without cause." He tapped the bowl of his pipe to clear it of ash. "Oh, well, I have made my decision. It's done, now. No looking back. I hate to do it but there's no alternative. I can't carry on as I am. These chest pains don't help."

He stood up, and running his fingers through his whitening hair, switched off the light and went through to the bedroom. He would confirm with Ben tomorrow about taking over from him.

Walking across to Helene's bed he seated himself at the foot so as to attract her attention. She opened her eyes in surprise at the unusual procedure.

Normally he crept in, undressed quietly and slipped into his own bed without making a sound. Tonight, however, when she was willing him to keep away from her he had decided to approach her.

The recent rebuke had made her deflated and miserable. It seemed as if no one but Wim understood her any more. Even her own daughter had begun to avoid her. There had been more tears. Tears of self pity.

"I want to talk to you." Edmund's hand went towards the bedside lamp.

"Don't put the light on. I have a dreadful headache."

"Very well."

She sat up painfully. Her heart was racing madly. She was terrified of an inquisition.

The light from the waning moon gave a dim glow to their silhouetted figures.

"You are trembling Helene. What's wrong?"

"I'm wondering what you are going to say. It must be important for you to sit on my bed," she said, with a trace of bitterness.

"Yes. It *is* important. I am leaving the hospital and taking you back to France."

Her reaction was immediate. "No, Edmund, no . . . you can't mean it!"

"I mean every word." He got up. "I have made my decision and there is no going back on it."

"No, no, no! You cannot!"

"But I can . . . and have."

Helene became hysterical. This was the final straw. She wept fiercely. "Oh, how horrible I am. To think that I have done this to you." She buried her face in her pillow and sobbed. "Edmund, darling . . . *please* don't give up the hospital. Let *me* go back with Suzanne and you stay on. No, no, no . . . I just cannot bear it," she wailed.

Edmund could not bring himself to take her in his arms and comfort her. She had already taken all his mental and physical strength in the unrelenting fight she had put up for so many years. Although he would care for her always, she had shut off his affections into a tight resentment. As he spoke the irrevocable words, he had the sensation of his purpose in life being taken from him.

Ever since they had come to Balandra he had borne her uncooperative attitude towards his work at the hospital. He could no longer stem his bitterness. He stood by the window for a time, letting Helene fight her own desperation, whilst the pain in his chest tore at him.

When, finally, she was a little quieter, he said, "I shall put arrangements in hand tomorrow. We will go back by sea, if it is possible."

At sun-up the following morning, after a sleepless night, Helene dressed quietly and got into her own car. She drove up to Wim's plantation and caught him just as he was leaving the bungalow to start work.

Her white, strained face told him that something serious had happened. He

hurried towards her and embraced her
without regard for who might see him.

She was shaking uncontrollably and
found difficulty in speaking, but managed
to get out, "He's taking me back to
France."

"When?"

"As soon as he can make the arrangements." Her voice me out in jerks. "I
cannot *think* what has made him do
this."

Wim held her close. "Come away with
me, my darling. Come now. This very
minute."

"Where?"

"We could go up to the Kapsabet. No
one would find us."

"Oh, if only we could . . ." She sighed.
"What about clothes?" she found herself
saying. "I must have some clothes."

"Go home and pack a bag. I'll call for
you in an hour."

It was almost as if they had rehearsed
it.

Helene returned to her home and
packed a suitcase. She stayed in her dressing-room until she saw the station wagon
then crept out without a sound. And

without a word spoken Wim got out and took her things, stowing them in the back. She got in beside him and they drove away.

It had been incredibly easy. Not even Suzanne had heard her leaving.

Now they could be together, at last. With no thought of any tomorrows.

The miles passed unheeded, the day was poignant. Never would she forget this journey. The wheels of the station wagon barely touched the road as sights and sounds around them gave her an intense awareness of the man beside her . . . the man whom she had loved for twenty years. It was like flying to heaven . . . where ever that might be . . . free . . . free . . . free . . . said the cool morning air as it rushed past them.

Wim turned to her, his blue eyes so very compelling.

She smiled at him with love in her heart, just as she had that long, long time ago. "I'll have to go back," she said.

"In a day or two, maybe," Wim replied. His voice was deep music. "But not for a while." Perhaps, now, he was hoping, I shall at last be able to persuade her to leave Edmund and remain with me.

When they arrived at the Kapsabet it was almost deserted.

The altitude was well above three thousand feet and the clouds were low. In the valleys and hills, permanent fine mist saturated the atmosphere. It gave them a feeling of dissociation from the rest of civilisation.

They walked into the hotel to find a roaring log fire in a large fireplace with a burnished copper hood. It was welcome after the chill outside. They wandered over to look at the intense green hills through the wide windows, and looking down, saw the trout stream as it followed the contour of the rise on which the hotel had been built. The music of the water broke the silence as it bubbled and gurgled between its undefined banks.

They collected the key to their accommodation and found it was a self-contained log cabin. The fire was ready set for lighting and there was a pile of logs beside it.

Wim knelt as he applied his lighter to

the dry twigs and the fire leapt into being. He got up and put his arm around Helene, and for a while they stood watching the flames.

In the firelight the shadows on the ceiling danced. The scent of the wood smoke and the gentle rustling sound of the flames enveloping the logs hushed the two lovers into quiet repose.

They would walk the rolling grassy downs together, where the turf was as springy as a thick thick carpet.

Recrimination would have to wait.

That same evening Helene telephoned Edmund at the hospital.

"I'm sorry, Edmund, but I needed to get away. I must think."

"Where are you?"

"Never mind that."

"I must know."

"There is no need. I shall be back again in a few days."

"Why can't you tell me where you are?"

"Because you would only come and take me away."

She is cruel, thought Edmund. He was shocked that she could behave so callously.

It reinforced his opinion that they would have to return to France.

A creeping doubt began to assert itself in his mind, but he refused to accept the possibility that she might be with another man. But what he could not understand was how she had left. Her car was still in the garage. Could she have telephoned for a taxi?

Suzanne, also, had her misgivings. "Shall we ask Claire if she knows, Father?"

"Do you think it possible that Claire might know?"

Suzanne shook her head. "I don't know, but we can try."

She telephoned Claire, but drew a blank. Somehow it didn't surprise her.

When her father left for the hospital next morning, Suzanne saddled Jason and rode up to Wim's plantation. She hoped he might have a clue as to her mother's whereabouts.

She tethered her horse and walked up the veranda steps and through into Wim's lounge. He was not there. It struck her that there was a feeling of emptiness . . . almost as if he had gone away for good.

Maurice appeared and she questioned him. He told her that Wim had gone away for a few days.

"Where?"

Maurice gesticulated with his hands. He didn't know. He appeared evasive, almost to the point of embarrassment.

She walked through to the bedroom wing. Something drove her on.

She went first to Wim's bedroom and threw open his cupboards. But she could tell nothing . . . he had so much . . . so many clothes.

On impulse she tried the door of the locked bedroom. It was open this time. She walked in. What a beautiful room it was. It was just as she had always remembered it.

She drew aside the filmy bed curtains and caressed the embroidered quilt.

Then something caught her eye . . . a pair of earrings on the table beside the bed. They jarred her, oddly. She wondered vaguely what they were doing there, for she recognised them as belonging to her mother. She looked around the room, then walked over to the wardrobe and flung open the doors. Some of her mother's clothes were folded neatly on the shelves, and hanging up was a dress she recognised.

Then the truth dawned . . . and she was horror-stricken.

She ran from the bungalow, her eyes unseeing and pain engulfing her.

She struggled up on Jason, kicking his flanks in her passion, yet clinging to him in her anguish.

"Oh Wim, *Wim* . . . how *could* you!" she cried.

10

HELENE and Wim had spent four days together, and Wim had decided that the time had come to discuss the future.

Sitting in the firelight on the couch, Helene waited for Wim to join her. But he was restless, walking about the room, not knowing how to begin what he had to say.

Helene, quick to sense his change of mood, said, "Is there something on your mind?"

"Yes, as a matter of fact, there is. One or two things."

Helene reached across and switched on the table lamp. "Tell me. What is it?"

Wim took a deep breath. "Let's discuss Suzanne, first."

"Suzanne! Why Suzanne?"

"Because she is unhappy, and it is you who have made her so."

"Wim!" She was at once astonished. Her eyes grew with disbelief that he could have said such a thing.

"Yes. You are shocked, I know. But I feel compelled to speak to you about her. You are not being fair to her, Helene."

"But what right have you . . . to discuss my daughter with me in such a way?"

"Every right. And you *know* it."

Helene blanched. Wim's words stung her. All these years and she had never told him! Yet he knew.

He said, gently now, "You are going to have to release her."

"Release her? She's not a prisoner."

"Then don't treat her as one. Let her go her own way. She'll come to no harm. In fact, she will be all the better for it—and love you all the more."

Helene was silent and rebellious.

"I hear on good authority that you intend getting her back to France, by hook or by crook."

"Who told you that?"

"It's common knowledge." He paused. "Can you not see how cruel you're being? This island is her home and yet you continually want to drive her from it."

Now she was crying softly.

"Don't cry, Helene. That won't put anything right."

"I . . . it's not that." Her voice was muffled. "It's the way you are speaking to me . . . as if you don't care for me any more . . . as if I am a stranger. I cannot bear it." She put up her hands to cover her face.

Wim played for time. He got up and went to a side-table to pour two drinks. A brandy for Helene, whisky for himself. He placed hers beside her on a small table, then sat down on a chair opposite her and looked down into his glass. After a suitable interval, he continued, "I guess I have said enough about Suzanne. Now we will talk about us." His voice had an edge to it that he had never before used to her.

Helene picked up her drink and sipped it then put it down hurriedly. "Us?" Her face betrayed an uneasiness, as if she knew very well what was coming.

Wim nodded. When he looked at her he could see the reflection of the flames in her dark luminous eyes. They were sombre, now.

"Just what does your marriage mean to you, Helene?"

She shrugged.

Wim stood up again. He wandered in

the direction of the window and stood looking out into the darkness as he spoke the fatal words. "I am going to ask you for the very last time, Helene. Will you leave Edmund and marry me?"

A smouldering end of log fell down into the embers and sent up a few hissing sparks. Then all was hushed as she said, in a voice that he could hardly hear, "I can't. It would be wrong."

"Not so wrong as the way things have been for the past twenty years." Wim felt weakened at his losing battle.

Looking towards the fire and shaking her head, she said, "There is something wrong with my whole life."

"There is something missing in most people's lives, but they have to learn to live with it."

"Not yours."

"Oh, yes. For all these years you have bound me hand and foot . . . and you don't even belong to me. When I think about that I feel pain."

"You could have married Merle."

"Don't be more cruel than you have to, Helene."

"Why are you saying these dreadful

things to me?" There was despair in her voice.

Wim walked slowly towards the back of the couch where she was sitting and reached over to put his arms around her from behind. He put his face against her cheek and could feel the tears that were falling unheeded.

"This is the end, my darling. The very end . . . unless, unless . . . you will promise to divorce Edmund and marry me."

"Oh, my love, please do not say it," she pleaded, clinging to his hands. "I *cannot* live without you . . . you *know* it."

"Then prove it," he said, gently releasing her. "I'll not ask you again."

The crates were piled up on the veranda, waiting for transport to take them to the quayside. They would wait there for a ship to get them to France.

Helene had supervised the packing of her desk, but that was all. No other possessions meant much to her. She gave little thought even to her clothes. The ones she had would suffice for the voyage, and the dresses she had ordered from Paris for

Suzanne were bundled into a tea-chest, unwanted by either of them.

She had returned to Edmund just as she said she would—early one morning.

At parting from Wim she felt a deep distress, and a dreadful longing for him returned again and again as an ache over her whole body. At these times she made an effort to reassure herself that her first duty was to Edmund and that remaining with Wim might not have worked. It was little consolation, but would have to do.

Mother and daughter now avoided one another to the point that Edmund must have noticed, though he said nothing.

Helene felt a great sorrow for her husband, yet was unable to remedy the now irreconcilable state of limbo between them. Perhaps I can make it up to him when we get back to France, she wondered, yet knew in her heart that it was now far too late for that.

Edmund went about his remaining tasks with an attitude of finality. What role he would fulfil at the château he could not imagine. He already felt obsolete.

Suzanne was inconsolable. Her anger at her mother's liaison with Wim even outweighed her grief at their home being broken up. She had always believed that hers was the special relationship with Wim. She knew now that whatever affection he had for her as a child it was because of her mother. She had a tight knot in her stomach whenever she thought of them together.

Helene tried to approach her, but Suzanne remained cold and indifferent. She blamed her mother for everything and found it impossible to forgive her.

"Father, *can't* you change your mind?" she begged him. "It's *terrible* to leave our home." She wondered if he knew the dreadful truth.

Edmund shook his head sadly. "It's no good, Suzanne. We shall have to get her back to France. She has never been happy here. I see that now."

"It would appear, then, that no one else's feelings matter," she said, spitefully. "You won't even be here for my birthday."

Her father was silent. He was sick at heart. There was nothing more he could say to her.

"Anyhow, I'm not coming back with you on the ship."

"You must please yourself." He felt ill. "What will you do?"

"Stay with Claire and Vincent until after Christmas."

"All by yourself."

"No. I shall have Erica."

"And then what?"

She shrugged. "I don't know. I shall have to think about it."

"Very well. I'll make financial arrangements so that you won't have to worry."

"Thank you."

The morning the lorry came to load the crates Suzanne decided she would ask Ben to take her things up to the farm. She couldn't face the prospect of seeing their household effects loaded up and carted away. Just as she was about to telephone him, however, Ben arrived to ask her if she would come into St. Louis with him. He wanted her to help him choose a parting gift from the staff, for her father.

"Can you give me any ideas?" he asked, as they were approaching the city.

"Oh, Ben, I'm *so* unhappy."

He stopped the car. "What is it? Your mother and Wim?"

"You know?" She was incredulous.

He nodded. "If only we could have prevented it. I did try to."

"You did! When?"

"On the trip into the mountains. *I* fetched your father. Did you know that?"

Suzanne shook her head. She knew very well that the trip into the mountains had not been the beginning: their relationship went much farther back.

"Your mother never forgave me," he added.

Suzanne's tears began to fall. Ben put his arms around her and she found herself crying on his shoulder.

"Please don't cry, Suzy. It was inevitable, you know."

"Why do you say that?"

He was silent.

"Please tell me why."

"Your father can never have been much company at home. He was never there: always at the hospital. Your mother told me."

She was thoughtful. "Come to think about it, we never *have* seen much of him.

Even as a child . . . I can't remember much about him at all."

"Oh well, a man can't be everything. He gave himself to his job. I suppose there wasn't much left over for his family. I hope I never get like that—obsessed."

"I'm sure he never realised. He loves Mother very much, you know."

"Of course he does. But, perhaps they are just a little too different. It sometimes happens when two people are from different backgrounds. They can never hope to understand one another completely."

"I think marriage is a silly arrangement." Suzanne was vehement. "I shall certainly never marry."

"Why do you say that?"

"Well, I think it's just a sham. People rush into it and then find they are stuck with someone for better or worse for the rest of their lives."

"Not everyone feels like that."

Suzanne shrugged. "I don't know about *other* people . . . I only know about my *own* parents." Her tone was bitter.

Ben turned to face her squarely, and

looking into her eyes, said, "Will you do something for me?"

"What?"

"Say 'yes'."

"Yes, then."

He smiled. "That's better. Dry those tears and come and help me choose that gift. I've had a very hard time trying to think of something original and all I can come up with is a fountain pen. He probably has one already."

"He wouldn't mind that."

They were both quiet for a while. Ben said, "I'm very pleased you are staying on for a while."

Suzanne was thoughtful. "Well, Father promised me I needn't do anything until after Christmas. Claire and Vinny don't mind having me. Then Erica and I can travel to England or wherever together. She's promised."

"You've become fond of Erica."

She nodded. "It's very hard to understand, sometimes."

"What?"

"Why things happen . . . I mean . . ."

"Would you like to come out with me this evening?"

She hesitated, remembering that the following day would be her parents' last on Balandra, perhaps for ever. Then she remembered how their whole family relationship had fallen apart. "Yes," she replied, "I'd like that, very much," and was grateful to him.

"Where would you like to go?"

"The Starlight Room, I think."

Ben smiled. He had not been planning such a gala evening, but he was pleased that Suzanne had made a suggestion.

"What are you grinning at?" she asked.

"The thought of my dancing. Are you sure you want to risk it?"

She gave a small laugh. "I'm no better."

When they reached the jeweller's they spent time over choosing her father's gift, finally deciding on a maroon fountain pen with a gold band. When the package was wrapped, Ben turned to her and said, quietly, "I should like to buy you something as a keepsake."

Suzanne felt her colour rise. His request was natural, yet she felt it was significant.

In his meticulous way Ben had already made a preliminary visit to select a gift.

Suzanne realised this as soon as she saw the assistant bring it from the showcase. It was a solid gold chain bracelet with a lock. She looked up at him, shyly.

"You like it?" he asked, hopefully.

She nodded.

"Let me put it on, then." He fastened it then looked at her intently as he raised his eyes from admiring the way it encircled her slender wrist.

"Thank you," she whispered. "It's lovely."

Ben was content.

When Suzanne and Ben returned to Spring Valley the crates had gone and so had Dr. and Mrs. Grayson. They had taken their luggage to the Landers' farm and would stay there until their departure.

The empty house looked forlorn. All that remained of the past was Helene's beautifully polished floors. Of Edmund there was nothing. Adele and Dudley were nowhere to be seen. They must have already departed for the new situation Edmund had managed to find for them.

Suzanne started to get out of the Pinto,

but Ben restrained her. "Don't go inside, Suzy. It will only upset you again."

She found she was obeying him. "Perhaps you're right. Anyhow, I can imagine it—I can't bear it. Let's go."

They drove off.

"Now, come along," he said, firmly. "It's a chapter in your life that is over. There is nothing we can do to change things."

Helene and Edmund sat in the small chartered aircraft ready for take-off. They were to fly to Martinique and board a cruiseship bound for France.

Helene was in the window seat and could see the faces of the six as they waited for the plane to taxi down the runway. She saw Suzanne looking tight-faced and reproachful. She had embraced her daughter, but Suzanne's response had been a mere formality. With Edmund, however, she had been more demonstrative, clinging to him and struggling to keep back the tears.

Now her eyes sought Erica. Somehow she had expected her to be standing close to Wim, but she wasn't.

She looked at Claire and Vincent. What a truly good couple they were. Why couldn't she and Edmund have been as happy and relaxed in their marriage? In all the years she had known them she had never heard them quarrel. Everything always seemed to be treated with humour, as if any situation could be resolved that way.

And now that they were at a safe distance she could no longer keep her eyes off Wim. He certainly wasn't smiling and she wondered what he was thinking. He could see her sitting at the window, but he didn't wave. Even as the plane moved off and taxied down the runway he didn't wave. Not once. That was her last sight of him. Now she would always have to remember him like that. She felt like a stone.

She turned to Edmund and touched his hand briefly, but he did not respond, even though he wanted to. The pain in his chest was almost unbearable.

This time she was more understanding, despite the fact that she had left her heart on the runway. "Have you brought those pills?" she asked, kindly, almost grateful for the diversion.

He nodded, reaching into his pocket, relieved that he could now take one openly without arousing her suspicions. "It is just as well we have said our goodbyes to the others now," he thought.

The five stood watching the plane until it was out of sight, then wandered silently back towards the vehicles.

Claire fished in her handbag for a handkerchief and blew her nose loudly and dabbed her eyes. She forced herself to be cheerful for Suzanne's sake. Vincent tucked his arm into hers and they did a kind of jog-trot across the parking lot. The sight of them fooling about broke the tension.

"Wait for *us*," called Erica, for once showing some spirit. She hurried after them, anxious to get away from Wim. As the plane had left the ground she had glanced at him, half hoping that he would seek her out, but she was astounded when she saw the raw emotion on his face. His guard had slipped and his feelings were plain. Compassion choked her as she shared his pain.

Before she realised what was happening, Wim got into his station wagon and drove off at speed.

The others crowded into Vincent's Range Rover.

Erica made a sudden decision.

"By the way, everybody . . . I think I should like a sea trip, too. So I'll be leaving just before Christmas. Is that all right with you, Claire?"

"Whatever you want to do is OK by me, love. But don't make it too soon, will you?" She squeezed Erica's hand affectionately.

Suzanne was upset. "You promised you would wait and go back with me."

"Yes, I know. I'm sorry, Suzy, but I've changed my mind."

"Why?"

"Well, there are several reasons. But the most important one is that I should like the sea trip. Actually, I felt very envious when I realised that Helene and Edmund were going by sea . . . I could have gone with them if I'd been quicker off the mark."

Suzanne paled. Erica's pronouncement was a blow to her.

But Ben thoroughly approved. "That's a very good idea, Erica. The sea trip will do you a lot of good. I wonder why you didn't think of it before."

"It never occurred to me. I came out by air, so I suppose I only thought in terms of going back that way. Yes, I like the idea. I shall really enjoy it."

Suzanne, completely silent, was acutely aware that there was nothing she could do about it.

11

EARLY the next morning, after a restless night, Wim rode up to the Landers' farm, leading the new pony, Sheena. He was surprised and pleased to find Erica waiting for him. Suzanne was nowhere to be seen. She was obviously still avoiding him.

Erica was wearing the same outfit she had worn on the trip into the mountains because it was so comfortable. Her chestnut hair was bobbing and blowing in the early morning breeze and her usually pale complexion was rosy. Wim could not but notice how charming she was.

"Were you shocked that I should be such a brazen hussy as to telephone you?" She smiled.

"I was pleased," Wim replied, quite seriously.

Wim held Sheena steady while Erica mounted. He gave her a quizzical look, not daring to ask if she was used to horses.

But Erica sat beautifully, which told him all he needed to know.

She flicked her whip and Sheena broke into a gallop, taking Wim by surprise: her confidence was very evident.

He jumped on to his own horse and galloped after her. She glanced back at him as they covered the distance, then suddenly she slowed to an easy canter and let Wim catch up with her rather than let him pass her, which he would certainly have done, if only to prove something.

As he came alongside, Erica threw back her head and laughed with sheer pleasure at having surprised him.

"I'm glad I never asked you whether you could ride," he said, wryly.

"Oh, Paul and I have been riding for years—ever since we were children. We often spend weekends in the country. With relatives."

They had come to some trees, a small wood, and about five hundred yards in was a fork in the track.

"*You* will have to lead," she challenged, "I don't know the way." Her face was radiant as she waited for him to give a sign.

Unexpectedly he dismounted and came to her side, holding on to her bridle. His expression was inscrutable. She looked down at him, not attempting to move or speak.

Wim saw her suddenly blanch and he became alarmed. He couldn't believe she was afraid of him. He tried to ignore her reaction and casually pointed to the way they would go, then let go of her bridle and remounted his own horse.

"I have never met anyone quite like you," he said. "You made me feel uncomfortable just then."

"Forgive me, Wim. It's something I can't talk about."

"There has been someone else in your life?"

She nodded. "I'm wary, now. Mistrustful, perhaps. I can't help it. I'm sorry."

"I had nothing sinister in mind."

"Please don't be angry. I *have* apologised."

They rode on in silence, but they both knew that a fragment of the high wall between them had fallen away.

The track led back through trees and

they finally came out into the sun on the hill high above Wim's plantation. Below them, the vast acres of coffee trees clothed the slopes with their dark polished green foliage. There was something so very efficient about the way the trees were planted—each one in its appointed place.

Far away, almost as far down as Wim's bungalow, Erica could see drying platforms and remarked on them.

"They are now mostly unused. We've gone over to mechanical drying—the machinery is in those adjoining buildings." He pointed. "Can you see where I mean?"

Erica nodded, and reined in her pony. Shading her eyes with her hand she looked back to the hills above and back again.

Wim regarded her steadily. "What are you thinking?"

"I was looking at the position of the sun." She hesitated. "The plantation is only in the sun for the first part of the day?"

"That's the general idea."

"One day I'll ask him about the whole process of coffee growing," she thought, "but not today."

"Shall we go?" he asked.

She nodded and smiled.

"Then follow me."

The coffee trees were at different stages of harvest, and he led her down the steep path which divided them. At last they reached the stables, where a groom was on hand to give the horses a rubdown.

Wim smiled at her. "You'll stay for breakfast?"

"I'd love to." Her mood had changed to friendliness, all restraint gone.

Wim led her to the cool veranda at the back of the bungalow.

Erica settled herself in a rattan lounger. "I suppose you were born here."

"Yes."

"Of Dutch descent?"

"Half. My father came here from Holland about forty-five years ago."

"What about your mother?" She hesitated. "Please forgive me for being inquisitive, but I'm interested."

"I don't mind telling you." He looked away to the left, across towards the mountains. "My mother died of yellow fever when I was very young. I don't remember her."

"I'm sorry," Erica said, quietly.

"She had never been strong," he continued. "My father missed her. It was very hard on him. They had so few years together, and from the little he spoke about her in his remaining years, she had meant everything to him."

Erica was silent.

Wim waved an arm in the direction of the plantation. "You know, he built up this outfit from almost nothing. The land was here, but it had been completely run down."

"Your mother. Was she English?"

"No. French. She came from Martinique."

"Then you have relatives there?"

"A few, but I don't often see them." He paused. "Ah, here comes Maurice with our breakfast."

"Mm . . . It smells delicious. I'm quite hungry."

To Erica, ham and eggs had never tasted so good. They ate leisurely, each pleasantly aware of the other.

"Tell me about yourself," said Wim, as he stirred his second cup of coffee.

Erica hesitated. "What would you like to know?"

"What ever you would like to tell me," he replied.

"I . . . I'm not sure where to begin," she said, slowly.

"Well, tell me first of all, what brings you here to Balandra."

She sighed. "Yes, I should like to tell you. I feel some explanation is due. . . you have been so kind . . ."

Wim said nothing. He waited for her to continue.

Erica was quiet for a moment or two longer, then taking a deep breath, said, "It's such an old, old story, it's ridiculous. But I suppose men and women will go on deceiving one another to the end of time." She put down her empty cup and rested her hands on the arms of the lounger, leaning back against the cushions.

"Someone I knew . . . a dress designer . . . asked me to model clothes at a show. They were to be of his own designs. He was new to the fashion world and hoped to get a foothold . . . not that I would ever blame him for that." She paused. "It was the way he did it." Another pause. "I was fond of him . . . fell in love with him . . . he asked me to marry him. Unfortunately,

195

the show wasn't a success and I lent him money to help him out of his difficulties. That was before I knew he already had a wife. Not only that, I found out that all the designs he had convinced me were his had been done by his wife. My whole world collapsed."

Wim said nothing. He didn't even move.

She went on, "I had a really bad spell. There were times when I felt I couldn't go on." There was a catch in her voice.

Wim's eyes roamed the distant hills.

Erica said, wistfully, "Paul has been so kind. This holiday was his idea."

Wim got up from his chair and walked across to the veranda rail and gripped it with both hands. "Tell me," he said, "what are your feelings for this man, now?"

"I feel nothing. Nothing at all . . . except a crying feeling somewhere inside me . . . that goes on and on and on."

Wim turned to face her, leaning against the rail with folded arms. "Yes, I do know how it is," he said, simply. "My own life hasn't been as I would have liked. Then changing the subject abruptly, he said, "I hear you have wasted no time in making your travel arrangements."

"Yes," she replied, sensitive that confidences had been exchanged. "I've managed to book a berth on the same ship that Helene and Edmund travelled on. It returns here in a month's time."

"Then you aren't going back to England immediately."

"Not immediately. I thought I might enjoy a trip down through Italy. It's something I've always wanted to do. Particularly to visit Florence. I have a friend there —a girl who was at modelling school with me. She's married now. To an Italian count, so I understand."

"I shall miss you."

"Thank you." She smiled up at him, now unafraid to meet his eyes.

On that bright memorable morning, when within each of them had been an unspoken ache, they had unexpectedly found solace in each other.

"Will you come tomorrow?" he asked.

"I'd love to," replied Erica.

When Erica returned to the farmhouse, Claire called to her from the kitchen.

"In here, love. Suzy's gone into St. Louis to do some shopping and meet Ben for lunch. Sit down and have a coffee with me. I want to talk to you."

Erica, flushed and happy from her rendezvous with Wim, smiled and said, "What about?"

"It's about Suzy. Ben has been on to me about her birthday. He reminded me that she would be eighteen on Sunday and wanted to know what I thought about his inviting her out for the day."

"What did you say?"

"I said, 'go ahead and ask her', and he laughed and thanked me."

"Do you think she will accept?"

"I don't know. But if she does, I think we ought to make the evening a special occasion don't you? It's a bit rotten for her with her parents gone. I do think Edmund might have waited until after her birthday. I think he could have done."

"What do you suggest?"

"Well, what about a family party of our own? I've been toying with the idea of a surprise party. What d'you think?"

"You mean, if she goes out for the day with Ben, we can get him to bring her back just after dark and we can all be hiding?"

"Something like that."

"I think that would be a splendid idea. How can *I* best help?"

"Well, for a start, tomorrow morning when you see Wim . . ." Claire looked up at Erica with a twinkle in her eye, "you can get him to promise to be here for the occasion. It just wouldn't be the same for Suzanne if Wim didn't come."

"Claire," said Erica, pensively, "have you ever noticed how much those two are alike?"

Claire gave Erica an old-fashioned look and said, "Yes, I suppose I have." She got up to pour herself a second cup of coffee.

Erica said no more.

When Suzanne returned later in the day, she said, casually, "Ben has asked me to spend the day with him on Sunday. Shall I go?"

"Why not, my love! It will be a nice change for you."

"I was a bit surprised when he suggested it."

"Oh? I think it's a good idea."

Suzanne looked down at her shoes. No

one seemed to have remembered that Sunday was her eighteenth birthday. She turned slowly and went towards her bedroom.

Claire winked at Erica. "No letting on, you understand."

Erica nodded and raised her hand. "I promise."

At nine o'clock on Sunday morning Ben called for Suzanne.

Still no comment had been made concerning her birthday and she had given up speculating. She was subdued, but pleased that at least she had an engagement for the day and wondered where Ben would take her.

He had suggested that she dress casually, so she had put on a new pair of pale blue denims and a white T-shirt, and carried a white knitted coat which she hoped would meet any eventuality.

She would have liked to ask Ben where they were going, but for some reason she was too timid to ask him. The non-recognition of her birthday had dampened her spirits. Fortunately, however, Ben appeared not to notice.

He was casual at first, and opened the car door for her as if he had been doing the same thing for weeks.

The Pinto moved off and Ben drove slowly until they were clear of the rough track leading away from the farm.

Neither spoke for some time, but eventually Ben decided he would begin a conversation by asking Suzanne if she had any idea where he was taking her.

"No. No idea at all. It's rather intriguing, I must say."

"Do you want me to tell you or would you rather be surprised?"

"Surprised, I think."

"Good."

Ben turned off the track on to the main road and put his foot down on the accelerator. The hood was down and the breeze caught at Suzanne's unrestrained hair. She opened her carry-all and took out a silk scarf to tie round her head, knotting it at the back as she had seen Erica do. She felt excitement rising and stole a glance at Ben. His attention was riveted on the road.

She couldn't help being aware of how handsome he was, and that in his off-duty slacks and shirt he had a debonair quality about him. His serious expression only served to endear him, for she knew him well enough by now to expect his sense of humour to erupt unexpectedly, to be followed by a roguish grin.

Soon St. Louis was well behind them and Ben was driving nearer and nearer to the harbour.

He gave her a quizzical glance as he slowed down and parked his car a short distance from the sea wall.

He opened the off-side door for Suzanne and she emerged expectantly. Ben pointed to a small sailing boat moored to a brass ring in the harbour wall. He beckoned Suzanne to follow him.

"I take it you are used to sailing."

She shook her head. "No."

If Ben felt surprise he didn't show it, though he found it hard to believe that someone who had spent her childhood on Balandra wouldn't have spent a great proportion of that time on the sea. Being such an island people, most families had access to a boat in some way or another, and when Ben had first arrived on the island, his one idea had been to own a boat.

He jumped on board and held out a hand to steady Suzanne. She followed his example, and though not nervous, she experienced a slight shock when the boat reminded her that she was no longer on dry land.

Ben certainly hadn't reckoned on Suzanne being a novice. He found her a comfortable seat and explained the rudiments of sailing, warning her to at all times keep clear of the boom.

She watched him run up the sails and a feeling of exhilaration caught her as the boat began to move. She was fascinated by the silence except for the sound of the water cutting past the hull. It was thrilling, and she told Ben so. He looked pleased.

"How is it that you haven't done this kind of thing before?"

"I don't know. I suppose I've never had the opportunity."

"But don't your parents *like* the water?"

"I don't know. My father, certainly, has never said one way or the other. He's always been at the hospital."

"Even on weekends or days off?"

"Oh, yes. And besides, I haven't been

here all that much. Every time I come home they can't wait to get me back to Europe again." She shaded her eyes with her hand and turned to look at the wake, her unconscious discontent dissolving in the mesmerism of the foaming white against the greeny-blue of the clear water.

Ben watched her for a while, then checked on bearings and wind, satisfying himself that all was well. The sail gave a small snicker of sound as he set the tiller against the breeze. Then he moved across to where Suzanne sat, her eyes still fascinated by the churning water. He sat down beside her.

She looked up at him. Her brow was smooth again and she laughed ingenuously.

Ben was unexpectedly moved to say, "Happy birthday, Suzanne."

Her eyes widened and a sparkle entered them. She flushed with pleasure as she gasped, "So you *knew!*"

"Yes. I knew."

"How?"

"That's my secret."

"I thought everyone had forgotten."

"Shame." His features gave way to that

beautiful smile she had come to look for in unexpected moments. It lifted her spirits. His brown eyes shone with pleasure as he realised his power over her mood. He held up a finger. "One moment, if you please." He got up and disappeared into the small cabin and some moments later emerged with a bottle of champagne and two tall tulip-shaped glasses.

"Hold these," he said, passing her the glasses to hold. Then he pulled the cork to an exciting pop and indicated so that he could pour.

Suzanne's mood had now changed to one of gaiety and she was quite caught up with what, in her limited experience, she considered a most glamorous occasion. She was thrilled.

Ben watched her face grow animated as she sipped her champagne. It was chilled to perfection. Once again he repeated the toast to her birthday, adding, "And may you find much happiness in the future."

She was radiant. "Oh, Ben! Thank you, thank you. I'll remember this day for ever." She held out her glass for more. But Ben poured her but a thimbleful. He was ever mindful of his responsibilities.

Slightly reckless, now, Suzanne said, "Where are we going?"

Ben replied. "Nowhere. Just round the bay." He smiled at her and watched for her reaction, but there was none but the pleasure of her acceptance.

At noon the daily shower of rain took them into the cabin, but it lasted only ten minutes or so and they emerged once more to enjoy the fresh, clean breeze and what had now become a circular tour. The harbour was at no time out of sight. Sometimes it was astern, at others starboard or ahead. The merry-go-round excursion appealed to Suzanne and she decided that it really was fun going nowhere.

About one o'clock Ben disappeared into the cabin and brought out a hamper. With arms akimbo he studied her, waiting for her to say something.

She smiled. "Food?"

He nodded, pleased that her reserve had disappeared. He opened the hamper and took out some large paper serviettes.

"When did you do all this?" she asked. "You must have come down early this morning."

He nodded. "I didn't want you to

know." He grinned at her as he proffered a box of chicken pieces, deliciously browned in southern-fried style in bread-crumbs, butter and spices. A companion box of mixed green salad was placed between them, plus buttered French bread.

Suzanne bit into a drumstick and raised her eyes. "Tastes heavenly," she said, then resumed munching.

Ben poured them a second glass of champagne and they drifted in ever varying circles whilst Suzanne's birthday moved through the blissful hours.

They talked of many things, and Suzanne found that she was confiding in Ben about her unsettled future. He said very little, merely encouraging her to say what was in her mind. At the age of twenty-eight himself, he considered that at eighteen a young girl is not always sure what she wants out of life. So he listened. Eventually she came round to talking about what she ought to do after Christmas.

"Never mind about what you *ought* to do, Suzanne. What would you *like* to do?"

She didn't answer him immediately, for

the voice locked deep in her heart cried, "Stay with Wim", but she had now come to realise that it could never be. That constant feeling had been with her since she was a small child, and she became aware, at that moment, that all childhood longings would have to be put from her. Suddenly she said, without thinking, "Ben, do you think I would make a good nurse?"

"What's the matter with studying medicine and becoming a doctor?"

She shook her head vehemently. "Oh, no, no. I just couldn't face up to those many years of study. Anyhow, I'm not cut out for it. I know that."

Ben was thoughtful. Finally, he said, "In that case, I think you would do well to go in for nursing. But you'd have to leave Balandra again. Are you prepared for that?"

She shrugged. "I'll have to be. I feel I want, at least, to do something worth while. That must come first."

Ben was pleased she felt so, but he didn't want her to leave Balandra. However, she was much too young for him to consider the alternative. She was so immature for her age: that was something else. He would have to be careful what he said.

"Nursing would certainly be worth considering," he continued. "Why not think about it over Christmas."

"Yes, I think I will. It's something I've always had at the back of my mind. I've only just realised."

"This is quite a momentous day in your life." He laughed, taking away the seriousness.

About six o'clock in the evening Ben rigged the sails for harbour. Suzanne, content as she had never before been, sighed. "I don't want the day to end."

"It isn't over yet," he replied.

Suzanne fell into reverie. She had loved every minute of her birthday. How nice Ben was. She watched him tidying the deck and stowing the hamper. Between them they had eaten every crumb of food and the empty champagne bottle had been ceremoniously dropped overboard.

They drove back to the farm in contented silence. The place was dark.

"Where is everybody?" Suzanne was puzzled.

"The place seems deserted." Ben was eager to preserve the illusion.

They got out of the car and walked in through the open door. It was dark except for the moonlight, which cast an eerie glow over the silent farmhouse.

Ben whispered, "Let me go in first."

Suzanne followed obediently. Her hand went towards a light switch but Ben restrained her.

"Sssh," he whispered. She could just make out his gesture of silence.

He sought her hand and led her gently to the centre of the living-room. Then he took both her hands in his, and for a split second Suzanne wondered if he was going to kiss her.

Suddenly there was a blaze of light and people were coming towards them— people they knew well. Claire, Erica, Vincent and Wim. Now they were all singing "Happy Birthday".

The table was set in buffet style and banked with flowers.

Quite bewildered now, Suzanne's eyes filled with tears of happiness. They had remembered, after all . . . all of them. It was a surprise party for her, and she loved every moment.

That night, when it was over and all her presents had been opened, she waited until Ben and Wim had departed, then went across to Claire and hugged her. She didn't speak. It wasn't necessary.

Suzanne lay in her bed, dreaming over the events of the day. It had been quite the nicest day of her life. She sighed with contentment, then turned on her side and closed her eyes. Sleep came easily.

The night before she left, Erica was in her room, making final adjustments to her packing. She had little to do as her baggage consisted mainly of the allowance for her outward flight from England. She could supplement her wardrobe on board. She was also sorting out her few souvenirs.

A weird-looking bird carved out of horn. She held it at arm's length in various positions, trying to decide how to place it to advantage, but ended up laughing at its odd appearance. "I'll give it to Paul," she decided. "It reminds me of him."

Her favourite souvenir was a large

salmon pink spider shell, its extended tines grown rigid with resistance against a million tides. She had found it herself when she and Suzanne and Paul had ventured out to the coral reef, which at low tide revealed itself like a half-submerged island. She slipped into reminiscence of that day, wishing that it could all happen again. How the boatman had taken them out to the reef, leaving them with a promise to return when the tide turned. Erica could still feel the excitement of treading warily on the crusty coral, feet in sea-saturated plimsolls for protection, and the ebb and now of the greeny-blue water.

She recalled Paul's anxiety as time went by and the sea crept higher, because the boatman was nowhere to be seen. He was certain they would be left to drown. Suzanne had never for one moment doubted that all would be well. The boatman came as the water rose to about eighteen inches and Suzanne, quite nonchalantly, beckoned him to pick them up.

Erica lifted the shell. It was heavy and must have weighed three or four pounds.

It was just as well that she was returning by sea.

Claire came in to see her. "Are you through yet, honey?"

Erica nodded, smiling.

"No regrets?"

Erica shook her head. "No, Claire."

"What about Wim?"

"Oh, Claire . . . I . . . he's much too in love with someone else."

"Then you know how it is."

"Yes. I know. I've known for a long time."

"What will you do?"

"I'm not sure yet." She ran her fingers over the pearly rose shell, then held it against her face. "I wonder if it has any secrets to tell," she said, moving it to her ear and listening, wistfully, half smiling as she did so.

Claire waited for a second or two, looking at the gentle auburn-haired girl with the gold-flecked eyes and wondering about her.

"Have you enjoyed your holiday on Balandra, Erica?"

"Oh, yes. Coming to this island has meant more to me than I can ever say."

She paused. "But I'm sorry that Suzy thinks I've let her down."

"She'll get over it, honey. Poor Suzy has a lot of adjusting to do yet."

Erica said, quietly, "I knew you would understand."

Erica left Balandra early the next morning. Wim went with her as far as Martinique so that he could accompany her to the docks and make sure she embarked safely.

They left in the same small aircraft that had ferried Helene and Edmund, and Erica felt strange that Wim should be seated beside her. She wondered if he was thinking about that other time and she turned to look at him. He responded with a smile that told her he was not.

Martinique harbour was brilliant in the glare of the afternoon sun. Erica stood at the rail of the ship while Wim leaned over it, looking down at the loading operations. He was very happy in her company and loath to leave her. They had about half an hour before visitors were ordered ashore.

"Thanks for everything, Wim."

He studied her face for a long moment

and found himself saying, "I wonder if we shall ever meet again?"

"I wonder."

"Will you write to me?"

She nodded. "Of course. It would be ungracious of me not to."

They parted reluctantly, as if they had only just discovered their friendship. She watched him walk down the gangway. At the bottom he turned and waved with both hands and remained on the dockside until the ship pulled slowly away and into the deep water channel to slide its way into the Caribbean Sea.

Erica remained at the ship's rail, watching Wim until he was out of sight. Then she gazed across the wide expanse of blue sea, knowing that with the healing of the old wound came a new longing . . . a deep yearning for the man who had shown her so much kindness in the past few months. Would she ever see him again?

She turned away from the rail and made her way down to her cabin.

12

A TRIUMPHANT Suzanne was admiring a batch of bread she had made under Claire's guidance. The four golden loaves were reposing on the wire rack in the farmhouse kitchen.

She had been intrigued at the way the potato yeast had worked, and Claire showed her how to leave a small quantity in the bottom of the large screw-top jar which would start the process for the next batch. Claire merely added a teaspoon of salt and one of sugar, plus six very thin slices of potato and half a pint of water. She screwed the top of the jar on tight and the warm climate would do the rest. Tomorrow it would be yeast again.

"Teach me some more things, Claire. Please."

Claire laughed. "OK, honey, what would you like to make tomorrow?" She walked over to a dresser and took a huge cookery book from the second shelf. "Here you are, my love. Have a go through that." She plonked it down on the table and Suzanne took it eagerly.

Claire commented, "I'm so relieved you're cheerful, Suzy. Vin and I have been a little worried in case you missed your parents."

"It's Erica I shall miss, not my parents. I just can't forgive Mother for taking my father away from Balandra."

"You've got it all wrong, Suzy. There was much more to it than that."

"Oh, I know all about her having an affair with Wim, if that's what you mean."

Claire was shocked. "I certainly wouldn't use *those* words."

"Well, what other words would you suggest? It's true, isn't it?"

"You don't know what love *is* yet, Suzanne. I think it's about time you realised a thing or two. Your mama has been a very lonely woman for many years. Wim knew that, and for years he has tried to be a comfort to her—and to you. You have only to cast your mind back to your childhood to realise what a good influence Wim has been."

"I hate you saying anything against my father."

"I haven't. But I *will. Now*. He has been no company at all to Helene . . . his work at the hospital has always come first . . . Wim knew that. Wim is a good man."

Suzanne bit her lip and looked down at the cookery book.

"I found Mother's earrings on the bedside table in Wim's bedroom."

"Whatever were you doing in Wim's bedroom?"

"It wasn't actually Wim's bedroom . . . I-It was another room he usually kept locked."

"I see," said Claire. "Then you are merely jumping to conclusions." She wandered back to her kitchen dresser, idly looking at the titles of other cookery books she had on the shelves. She was disturbed at Suzanne's callous attitude towards her mother. She turned to see Suzanne watching her intently. "Had you never noticed what an obsession your papa always had for his work? Never noticed how weary he always was? Just driving himself?"

"Yes, of course I did. I even spoke to Mother about it. But she didn't seem to care."

"Of course she did."

"Oh, Claire, it's so difficult to understand people." She looked down at the cookery book.

"Nobody would expect you to understand, love. Even your mama. She would never hold it against you."

"I don't think I'll ever forgive her for taking Wim away from me."

"But she didn't. He has always loved you both."

Suzanne's eyes filled with tears and she sat down at the table again, leafing through the large cookery book and trying to come to terms with what Claire had just told her.

"Let's make a lemon pie, shall we?" Claire picked up the large book and replaced it on the shelf. "It's one of Vinny's favourites."

Suzanne got up from the table and browsed along the shelf to pick out a smaller volume.

And then the telephone rang.

Claire answered. She turned to Suzanne. "It's Ben," she said. "He's coming up to see us."

"What about?" Suzanne was mildly curious.

"It seems he's had a cable from France."

"From Father?"

"No. Your mama."

"Why couldn't he tell you about it over the telephone?"

"I don't know, honey." Claire had a small frown between her brows. "We'll just have to wait and see." They waited. It was half an hour later when Ben arrived. He got out of his car with great deliberation and walked slowly across to the farmhouse. Claire was shocked when she saw his expression. He was clearly the bearer of bad news.

She put a hand on his arm and led him in to where Suzanne sat at the table still engrossed in the cookery book she had taken from the shelf.

Ben sat down opposite her and clasped his hands, resting them on the table. He looked unhappily at Suzanne.

"What is it, Ben? Tell me."

He shook his head slowly from side to side. "I just can't say it any other way."

"Say what? Tell me." Suzanne was becoming agitated.

"It's Dr. Grayson. He died this morning. A heart attack."

Suzanne didn't speak. Claire went quickly to her side and placed a sympathetic arm around her, but Suzanne shook it off and walked from the room.

"I hated being the one to tell her, Claire, but it would have been cowardly of me to wait and let Wim do it. It doesn't change anything."

"Wim isn't here, anyway," she replied, automatically. "He's in Martinique, seeing Erica off."

Ben got up. "There's no use in my hanging around. I'd better get back. I'll come up again tomorrow, and see if there is anything I can do to help."

Claire patted him on the shoulder. "Thanks. It was a pretty unpleasant task for you. I'll do what I can. Vinny will go over and get Wim when he gets back from Martinique. He should be back some time later this evening."

Ben walked back to the Pinto and drove away. It was done, now. Dr. Edmund

Grayson had died, and it had been no surprise.

Helene had come upon her husband in a corner of the walled garden where he had taken to sitting and reading. The book lay open on his lap and he appeared to be asleep. He had known no struggle, and for that Helene was grateful. His life was over. The man who had been her husband: a man who had never said an unkind word to her.

Her thoughts went back to the moment on board when he had spoken of the voyage being beneficial to them both, and his words had proved prophetic. The leisurely days had engendered a new depth of feeling neither had previously experienced. Helene was well aware that it had been companionship she had craved for so many years, but even though she explained this to Edmund he had never really understood her need. Locked in his own well-ordered and logical world it had never once occurred to him that his wife's pattern of life was different from his own and that her heart was just as vulnerable. That he had never understood the depth

222

of her passionate nature had been their misfortune.

And now . . . nothing remained of him but those few recent happy memories of shared moments on board ship. Helene was appalled when she considered her life in retrospect: of her frustrations over the past twenty years. Her jealousy of Edmund's work at the hospital now revealed itself as such a futile emotion, and in its wake came a relentless remorse.

Wim left Martinique with misgivings. Though he was now free to pursue his life again he suddenly remembered that nothing could ever be the same again now that Helene was gone. She had been a constant companion since he was eighteen. Their youth had slipped away like bubbles rising from the seabed.

He thought about her, trying to picture her on the voyage back to her beloved France, speculating on what the future would hold for her. Would she be content now? Would she *ever* be content? "I wonder," he thought, "All I know is that she is gone from me for ever. Lost. Never again will I possess her, even for one hour of a single day in a whole lifetime from now on. It is as if she has died," he despaired.

He ploughed his way up the long stretch of road which only that morning he had travelled so lightheartedly with Erica, admitting to himself that he would miss her.

As he finally drew up outside his bungalow he saw Vincent's Range Rover parked, with Vincent sitting behind the wheel, waiting for him. He knew at once that something was wrong. Vincent's white, strained face confirmed it.

"Is it Edmund?" Wim found himself asking, without knowing why.

Vincent merely nodded. "Will you come over tomorrow? Suzanne is beside herself."

"I'll come now. Wait. Just let me have a wash. It has been a long day."

Wim sat beside Vincent in the Range Rover and they drove over in silence except for Vincent giving Wim the brief details. They knew only what the cable had said. "You had better stay the night," added Vincent.

When they reached the farm Wim got out of the passenger seat and walked into the farmhouse. Claire met him in silence and led him to Suzanne's bedroom door. He tapped lightly and walked in.

She was huddled into a tight, convulsive posture.

He went quickly towards her, saying, "Suzy, darling." And taking her in his arms he comforted her and she clung to him desperately. All the pain he had caused her was forgotten in her distress.

As he consoled her he discovered a deep tenderness he had never before experienced. It was as though Suzanne was comforting *him* instead of the other way round. In some mysterious way she had become the mediator between Helene and himself. She was truly his daughter, and yet she might never know.

He held her close until her grief was spent and she had relaxed a little. Then he laid her head on the pillow and smoothed her tear-damp hair from her face.

"Sleep now, Suzy," he said, "I'll be here tomorrow."

Then he covered her with the light quilt and went quietly from her room.

"Come *here*, you rascal!"

225

It was three weeks later, and Suzanne was trying to coax the recently acquired Dalmation puppy out of the turkey pen.

"All right, then! I won't throw you any more sticks to fetch," she threatened, backing away slowly as the puppy, still with his head cocked to one side, was trying to anticipate her next move. He was far more interested in Suzanne then the turkeys, but he liked their funny antics every time he ran towards them, and Suzanne couldn't help but laugh when their wattles turned completely white with fright. "Oh, those poor turkeys!"

"And just what is going on here?"

Suzanne spun round. It was Wim.

The puppy immediately abandoned the turkeys and rushed at him. Suzanne, somewhat shyly, said, "Hello. It's been ages. Where've you been?" She involuntarily ran to him, forgetting for that split second all that had gone before. When she remembered she looked down at the dog, her cheeks flaming.

Wim bent down to pet the puppy. His face looked drawn. "I hear you are leaving in a few days. I thought I'd come and see how you were."

Suzanne managed to regain her composure, saying, "I'm OK. Claire and Vinny let me do as I like." But an ache was coming into her throat.

"Oh, they do, do they!" He made an effort to grin, betraying that he was aware of her discomfiture.

Suzanne, calmer now, but with a slight catch in her voice, tried to speak lightly. "I picked ten pounds of guavas this morning."

"So you are learning to be useful."

"Um." She nodded. "I miss Erica, though," she added.

"Did you have a good Christmas?"

She nodded. "Quiet, though. None of us felt like celebrating much."

"I hear you have decided to go into nursing."

"If they'll have me."

"When do you start?"

"I'm not sure yet, but I believe about halfway through February."

"Where?"

"Ogbourne Street."

"Are you planning to go over and see your mother first?"

"I'm not sure yet. I'm going straight to

Cornwall. Anyhow, Erica is there. They don't need me."

"Erica is in France?"

"Yes. She's staying with Mother."

"I'm pleased to hear that."

She looked up at him, anxious to avoid the subject of her mother. "Wim, do you think Father was very upset to leave the hospital?"

"Of course he was. But I also think it was wise for him to do so. He should have eased off long ago. He worked much too hard. Long hours."

"Well, so do you."

"Yes, but I'm different. Mine is physical work mostly, and physical work is self-limiting. Edmund's responsibility at the hospital was too demanding on him."

Suzanne paused. "Mother always said he spent too much of himself on the hospital. I never knew what she meant until now. Do *you* think that?"

"Yes, I'm afraid I do." He looked down at the puppy trotting meekly at his heels.

"He wouldn't do that for me," said Suzanne.

"She's not serious enough, is she, Dizzy!" He looked down at the dog. It would have obeyed any command from Wim.

"Well," said Suzanne, "how can I be serious with such a rascally creature? Just look at him. He's quite mad. Or stupid. I can't decide which."

They laughed together and went towards the farmhouse, where Claire was standing in the doorway.

As they walked across to her, Suzanne turned to Wim. "Will you have Jason for me, please Wim?" She bit her lip.

"Certainly. I would have in any case. But keep him until you go."

Inside the farmhouse he stood pensively revolving his hat on one hand. With the other he fingered the band, seeking the join.

"Well, I must go," he said. "Must get back before dark. There's a job I have to do." Then he addressed Suzanne. "How about coming for a ride with me tomorrow morning, early?"

"Yes . . ." She hesitated only a fraction before she added, "please. I've been quite jealous of your rides with Erica."

"Well," he shrugged, "it was up to you. You were welcome to come with us."

But after he had made the remark he wondered just how honest he had been.

The station wagon moved swiftly along the road towards the airfield.

Suzanne glanced at Wim as she sat beside him. His strength and reassuring presence filled her heart with gratitude as he steered the vehicle on to a fairly level patch of ground. He braked and turned to her. "This is it, then."

She turned to face him, her blue eyes dark and still troubled by the events of recent months.

Wim patted her hand as it lay between them on the seat.

Suzanne looked across the airfield as she said, "I feel a bit unkind because I refused Ben's offer to bring me out, but I wanted *you* to see me off. He was disappointed."

"It was best this way. He'll understand." His eyes were focused on the aircraft as it taxied into position.

"No . . . I suppose not . . . although . . ." It was almost a whisper. "He has been very kind to me since my parents left. I like him so much."

There was a pause.

"You are quite sure you still want to go?" Wim watched her expression with concern.

"What choice do I have?" She shrugged, then took a deep breath. There was bitterness in her voice. "I no longer have any family here. What's the point of staying." Her remark was rhetorical.

Wim said nothing.

She glanced over ther shoulder, reluctantly. "How long before. . . ?"

"There's plenty of time." Then placing his hand over hers again, he said, "Never forget, Suzy . . . You can come back any time you wish. There will always be a home for you at the plantation."

A long silence ensued. Then, hardly trusting herself to speak, she opened her overnight bag and took out a small red leather diary. "Look," she said. "See what I wrote just before I left England."

Wim took the diary from her and read aloud:

"Tenth of March. Going home."

He waited a moment, then closed the diary carefully, without comment, and gave it back to her. As she returned it to her bag he saw a tear fall. To cover her emotion she began checking on her belongings. Then she spoke again.

"Wim, may I ask you something?" Her voice faltered.

"Ask away." His hand involuntarily adjusted the driving mirror. He was afraid of what was coming.

She swallowed. "Do you still think of me as a child?"

He took his time.

"Do you?" she repeated.

Finally, he turned to her. "You will have to work that one out for yourself, Suzy."

She was silent.

"Think back over the years," he went on. "Think about your childhood. It should tell you something."

"About you and Mother, you mean?"

"Yes." He knew that this was the time to tell her the truth, but found he could not. "Will you go over and see her?" he asked.

She shook her head, still blinking away the tears that misted her eyes and would not go. "Not yet . . . I can't . . . perhaps . . ." But she never finished the sentence.

Wim said, "How would it be if I came over to see you later in the year?"

Suzanne looked up at him quickly and their eyes met. His remark was unexpected. "Would you?" She caught her breath as she spoke.

"I might," he said, grinning at her as he had so many times in the now remote past.

A flush of pleasure came into her cheeks. "I should love it," she replied.

"There's a condition." He didn't look at her.

"A condition?"

"You'd have to spend a holiday with me . . . with us . . . in France." Then he turned to look at her.

Her eyes opened wide and her colour receded. "You mean . . . with *Mother?*"

He nodded.

Her lips tightened. "I see." She looked down at her hands and a feeling of overwhelming confusion rose within her.

Wim got out of the station wagon. "Come now," he said, gently, and went round to open her door.

They gathered her luggage together and walked towards the waiting aircraft.

Seated in the small plane that would take her to Trinidad, and thence by jumbo jet to England, Suzanne turned to wave to Wim.

She could see him standing beside his station wagon.

He acknowledged her wave, then as she lingered on the top step, she saw him take out a cheroot and light it, one foot on the bumper, the arm holding the cheroot resting on his knee.

She gave a final wave, then entered the aircraft and passed along the gangway to take her seat by a window. She had every intention of preparing herself mentally for the journey, but a hopeless, lost sensation closed in on her, and she felt as if she were drowning in the desperation of having to leave the country of her birth. It was so final, and so unlikely that she would ever see Balandra again.

The stewardess glanced at her and wondered at her pallor. She looked up and gave a wan smile.

The stewardess spoke. "Can I help you put away your coat?" she asked, kindly.

Suzanne handed it to her, automatically murmuring thanks.

"Are you feeling all right?"

"Yes, thanks." Suzanne clenched her fists. "I must not give way," she told herself.

"Is there anything I can get you?"

Suzanne shook her head.

The stewardess, uncertain, said, "Well, anyway, I'll be back a little later on. After take-off." She bent down and solicitously buckled Suzanne's seat-belt. "There." She smiled and was gone.

Suzanne stared out of the window. She could see nothing but a large expanse of wing. It was at that moment she admitted to herself that the agony of departure would have to be endured.

13

WITH her arrival at Heathrow now behind her, Suzanne boarded the Cornish Riviera Express at Paddington and settled herself for the long journey ahead.

On the way, she questioned herself as to why she felt so reluctant to return to Cornwall. The prospect of sharing her grandparents' grief was painful to her. The wound would open up again. But her affection for the two old people who had done so much to make her schooldays so pleasant had bound her to them. She owed them so much, and now she convinced herself that they needed her.

She looked out of the window at the English April countryside, but though she admitted it was beautiful it didn't gladden her heart as it had the previous time she had travelled down to Cornwall. Disappointment clouded her vision and she turned away to open the magazine on the seat beside her.

At Truro station she found a taxi to take her to Pellisk, a bare mile and a half away, and as she sat back watching familiar scenes she was surprised that they held no joy for her. A numbness had seized her spirit, and as the taxi-driver turned up the long steep fir tree-lined driveway of her grandparents' property she had the sensation of travelling into a long, dark tunnel from which there was no escape.

She paid the taxi-driver and picked up her case, merely glancing at the front door of the cottage. She walked round the side, past the grassy banks that were studded with orange and mauve polyanthus and in through the outhouse. She stepped back in time as she saw the trays of eggs set out on the wooden bench and, in the corner, the old Thor washing-machine which would trundle through next Monday's wash.

The back door was open, as she knew it would be. She trod lightly across the large homely kitchen, and as her grandmother turned to greet her she put her arms about her and held her until the tears had been blinked back and the ache in her throat was under control. Even so, she found it difficult to speak and it wasn't until her grandmother kissed her that she found her voice.

"Where's Gramps?"

"Up in the orchard. He's been there since early this morning. Pruning that large Bramley."

Old Mrs. Grayson s pale blue eyes held a look of incomprehension. It was obvious to Suzanne that she had not yet fully realised that her only son had died.

Although it had been only a year since Suzanne had seen her last, Mrs. Grayson's frailty had enhanced and her hands were less steady, but her soft white hair still curled about her kindly face, and Suzanne was reminded that at least the two old people had each other.

"Tell him I'm making the tea. That should fetch him." She patted Suzanne's arm as if she had never even left.

Suzanne ran willingly up to the orchard, passing the chicken run as she did so. The clumps of stinging nettles were still entangled with the long grass against the wire netting and the chickens were still stalking about the orchard as they had always done. She recalled her responsibility for locking them up each night and smiled to herself at the memory of the night she had accidentally left one out and it had had to perch on the top of the henhouse all night. The following morning when she had gone up to feed them it had run towards her, squawking and flapping its wings accusingly.

It seemed that life here went on regardless of the outside world. Perhaps it was just as well. For old Mr. and Mrs. Grayson the security of their own world was all they could grasp now that they were ageing fast.

"Gramps! I'm back. Tea's ready." She could see him up in the far corner of the orchard. He was oiling one of his saws. He turned and stood watching her as she climbed the steep slope towards him. He dropped his oily rag and put down his oil-can to offer her his bearded face to kiss. He smelled of tobacco and ripe apples.

"Hello, m'dear. You'm got here safe and sound then."

She nodded happily and they strolled down to the cottage together.

Tea was bread and butter and two kinds of jam, as always. Watercress in a glass dish, and a jar of fish paste, with fruit cake to follow. A dear familiar routine, and it quietened Suzanne's troubled heart. Nothing was said, then, about Dr. Grayson, yet they were all aware that during the next few days the time would come when his name would enter the conversation. And so it was.

One morning, two or three days later, her grandfather said, quite casually, "You know, m'dear, Edmund went away a long time ago. It was then that we lost him. Not now. But he was always a good son. Someone we had faith in. He did his best always. Now we'll let him be. Eh?" He met her gaze. Suzanne nodded, and that was how she finally accepted her father's passing. The way her grandfather had.

The time came for her to go. She left them with a promise to return in a few months. They said goodbye as they did everything now—with resignation.

Suzanne had found a new freedom. A beginning again, and she hoped it would remain with her. She would remember the orchard, and the spring, and it would remind her.

14

SUZANNE stretched out a sleepy arm to quieten the alarm clock on her bedside table, then turned her back on it. But only for a few moments. The fact that there was no sun coming in through the window reminded her where she was and she sat up, bringing up her knees and tucking the blankets round her legs for a few precious seconds.

Her dreams had been crowded, as usual, but she could remember nothing distinct about them except for a vague disquiet which often remained with her throughout the day.

It was now May, two months since her introduction to hospital life.

The hours flipped by in a never-ending whirl of activity between shifts. She felt like a leaf blown about in a rough wind: a wind that never permitted her to settle for a single brief adjustment.

She supposed she would get used to it, given time. At least it dulled the pain of her absence from the island she loved and prevented her from remembering that she now had no family, for she had fallen into the habit of disregarding her mother. Could it really have been only a year since she had so eagerly stepped from the aircraft into the bright sun of Balandra with her heart full of happy anticipation for the future?

She gave a quick resigned sigh, then pushing back the bedclothes, swung her feet to the floor, wincing as they touched the chilly linoleum.

She hunted for her sheepskin moccasins, then slipped her feet into them and moved across to the wash-basin to splash her face with cold water. She poured some into a tumbler to clean her teeth. Even the water tasted different. She shuddered. "And it's so cold," she muttered. "Ugh!"

She pulled the bobbled cord of the light which illuminated the mirror over the wash-basin and studied her appearance.

"I even look different," she said, aloud, running her fingers through her shining hair. The long curling waves that had reached almost to her waist were gone. It was now just plain bobbed. Still, she considered, it has been a good idea. No fuss now, and so easy to manage under my cap. She shook her head vigorously and her hair fell back into place. She acknowledged her reflection with a half-hearted grin.

She still retained the habit of giving her hair a few strokes with her old ebony-backed whalebone brush, the one she had always carried with her, wherever she went. The memory of expensive silver-backed brushes on an elegant dressing-table was still with her, and for a brief instant she thought of her mother. But it was still painful to do so.

Sometimes memories of the past year would protrude into her day, but she would push them back with all the willpower at her command. Bitterness was a constant threat, and she was aware that there was a danger it would engulf her if she so much as gave way to it, even a little. No, she told herself, bitterness must *not* creep in. She must fight it with determination. It would get her nowhere . . . and yet . . . how could she ever forget what her mother had done? She turned away from her thoughts and concentrated on dressing.

After she had put on her snowy starched apron, she pinned on her cap. She made her bed, glanced over the room to make sure it was tidy, then opened the wardrobe and took out her dark cape with its scarlet lining and put it around her shoulders. There was something comforting and protective about it.

Closing the door behind her, she walked briskly along the corridor, her new leather shoes emitting a faint squeak.

She went first to the post-rack. There were two letters for her. One from France, which she tucked into her pocket, and the other bearing a West Indies postmark. The second she kept in her hand: she would read it at breakfast.

She walked on until she came to the glazed walkway that led from the nurses' flats to the main hospital building. She heard running footsteps and turned. Her flatmate caught up with her.

"Hi, Suzy! What's your hurry? Why didn't you wait for me?"

"I'm starving," she replied, laughing

good-naturedly. The two girls entered the canteen and found a vacant table.

Jill grinned across at her. "A letter from your beau?"

Suzanne smiled and shook her head. "But d'you mind if I read it?" She hoped it might be from Wim, but she didn't recognise the handwriting.

"I wouldn't dare say 'no'." Jill laughed and stood up. "I'll get our food. What d'you want?"

Suzanne shrugged. "Oh, anything. Whatever you're having will be fine."

Jill went across to the counter and Suzanne opened her letter. An expression of pleased disbelief spread over her face. She would read it later. She hastily folded the pages and returned them to the envelope, smoothing it out and tucking it carefully into the front of her uniform.

Jill brought scrambled eggs. "Eat," she commanded, "you're getting thin. We can't have you wasting away before our very eyes." She plonked down the plates. "You can get the coffee. That is, if you've finished reading your love letter."

Suzanne flushed. "Righto," she said, and got up to collect two coffees.

For the remainder of the day Suzanne's mind dwelt on the contents of the letter she had been so delighted to receive, and it was only when she came off duty that evening when she remembered the other letter, the one from France.

She opened it cautiously, thinking it might be from her mother, but it was from her Uncle Pierre, asking her if she would be coming over. He thought she ought to see her mother.

Suzanne crumpled the letter in her hands, then opened it out again, shaking her head. 'What *am* I to do?' Then she stuffed it back in her pocket, uncertain and unhappy.

That same evening she had a date with Paul. She wasn't keen on meeting him again, but it had been difficult to refuse him. He wanted to take her somewhere special, he said.

If Suzanne had received her letter sooner she would have cancelled the date. As it was, she felt obliged to let it stand. She would have to tell Paul she didn't want to see him again when they said goodnight.

It made her feel guilty. It seemed a mean thing to do.

He called for her at eight o'clock, at the flat she was sharing with Jill on a temporary basis. He had motored across London in his new white Ferrari, and planned to take Suzanne down to Richmond for dinner.

Jill opened the door when Paul rang. She was intrigued to meet the tall, elegant young man who was Suzanne's date, and it was a mystery to her why Suzanne was rather half-hearted about her evening. Yet he appeared undismayed, and chatted amicably with Jill while he waited patiently for Suzanne to put in an appearance.

Suzanne finally emerged. She had taken trouble over her appearance and looked radiant.

The letter she had received that morning had been read again and again. It was all she could do to prevent herself from replying to it immediately, but it would be delicious to think about for a day or two.

Paul was very cheerful that evening, and Suzanne at her most charming. Paul was led to believe she viewed him with favour.

They drove down to Richmond to an expensive hotel beside the river, and with their extravagantly delicious dinner they drank a whole bottle of champagne between them.

Towards the end of the meal Paul asked her whether she was homesick. He realised as soon as he had done so that it had been unwise of him. However, Suzanne remained unmoved.

She said, "I try not to think about it."

Was it his imagination, or was there a sudden flash of something in her eyes . . . as if it no longer mattered?

The subject was dropped and they continued to enjoy their evening. Suzanne had an inner glow about her, something Paul had never seen before. Could it possibly be that she had begun to care for him? Perhaps even love him? He began to view the future with optimism.

After the meal they danced, and it was one-thirty in the morning when they began the drive back. By now the weather had changed, and a fine misty rain was falling. Paul put up the hood and they drove in contented silence.

Sitting beside Suzanne he was unable to

resist touching her hand, wanting to hold it.

For a brief moment Suzanne responded, but it wasn't long before she let it go on the pretext of pulling her cape more closely about her.

Paul felt discouraged, but determined not to give up. Perhaps if they made another date . . .

"Why doesn't Erica get in touch with me?" Suzanne had suddenly shifted the evening into another dimension.

Paul hesitated, somewhat taken aback.

"She's rather busy at the moment. Re-establishing her career. But she will, soon, I feel sure."

"She *is* back from France, I suppose!"

"Yes. She got back a week ago. As a matter of fact she spoke of you only yesterday. We discussed a suggestion of Erica's that you might like to come down to Sussex with us for a long weekend. My aunt has a place there. Horses, and there is fishing, or we can walk, if you would prefer."

"Sounds good." She paused. "But I'm not sure when I'll be free again." Her tone was discouraging.

"I see."

By now they were almost back at the hospital, and for the remainder of the journey there was a chilly silence.

The car drew up and Suzanne lingered. She had something else to say to him.

"Paul," she began, "it's very difficult for me to say this after you have given me such a wonderful evening, but . . . well . . . the thing is, there is someone else. I'm sorry."

Paul gripped the steering-wheel and stared into the distance, where the headlights illuminated the empty street. He swallowed hard. "May I ask who?"

She shook her head. "I'd rather not say at the moment."

"Thanks a lot," he snapped. His voice held a note of sarcasm. "Then it's 'goodnight to you, Paul, and the best of luck'," he added, now flippant and angry.

"I'm truly sorry."

She got out of the car and waited a second or two for him to speak, but he only said, "It's goodbye, then," and reached over to slam the car door. His mouth was set in a hard, straight line.

Suzanne stood in the rain, listening to

the harsh revving of the engine as he drove away. He was furious. Then she sighed and walked into the hallway of the flats.

"He could at least have seen me to the lift," she thought. "That proves what I've felt all along. He's not for me."

Several evenings later, Suzanne sat on the edge of her bed and replied to Ben's letter. She found it was easy to write simply and clearly how she felt. She told him that she had been delighted to hear from him and would very much like to hear all about what had been happening in Balandra since she left.

Ben replied within a few days, and during the ensuing weeks and months an intimate correspondence grew between them.

Ben's letters were solemn for the most part, yet displayed often that sudden flash of humour which Suzanne had come to love.

She enjoyed having her letters sent to the hospital. It gave her a secret pleasure to hunt through the letter-rack for the now familiar handwriting and the West Indies postmark.

15

I N late May, some distance from Ogbourne Street, Erica was riding in a taxi on her way to the fashion house which had first figured in her career. But the nearer she got to her destination the less inclined she felt towards renewing her acquaintance with old colleagues. Yet she was well aware that it was inevitable if she wanted to carry on in the same line of business. Her only consolation was that the man who had caused her so much unhappiness had gone away. He was now in America.

The day was sunny, and she was wearing an olive green shirt dress cut on safari lines. Somehow it appeased her mood of latent dissatisfaction. There was, she sighed, so much missing in her life now. It had no purpose and there was so little to look forward to.

When she had left France she returned to London to stay with her brother in his small mews house. He had always been kind to her. But although she knew Paul was content for her to remain with him, she found it increasingly difficult to settle back into any kind of routine.

Having become involved with the Graysons as a result of their holiday in the West Indies, Erica longed to return there. She also knew that it was Wim who was exerting the strong pull on her longing to go back. But to return alone was impossible. It was all very well to go there as a visitor: it was another matter to make a way for herself on her own. She therefore had no alternative but to pick up the threads of her old life and begin all over again.

She had also developed an insatiable appetite for travel. It had stemmed partly from the excitement of their experiences on Balandra and partly from her reluctance to face the future. Travel had served to dull the remnants of her past disillusionment, and helped her to meet people and enter their lives for a brief spell without involvement. And yet involvement was what she craved.

She thought constantly of Wim, and could still see his face as Helene was borne away from him in the charter plane on its way to Martinique and the ship back to France. Her compassion for him was absolute.

When she had arrived at the château on her way back from Italy, Helene had been grateful for her companionship in her hour of bereavement, and in a single intimate conversation had confided in her. It had come out as a cry of desperation, and Erica had marvelled at Wim's devotion over so many years when he might have had a wife of his own, and could have, so easily. Any woman would have jumped at the chance.

Erica sighed and made an effort to turn her mind away from Wim, but it was not easy. Just as Helene had loved him, so did Erica. But Erica's love was selfless. Her feelings for him at times were almost maternal: he brought out in her a yearning to offer him complete and utter devotion as a means of consoling him in his desertion by Helene. For that is how Erica saw Helene's behaviour, admitting to herself with some discomposure and intensity of feeling, that Helene had been selfish in the extreme. And not only selfish, but possessive.

Whilst Erica had been staying at the château, Helene began to withdraw into herself, so that as the weeks went by and there was no improvement, there was not much point in staying on.

Erica knew that it was nothing to do with her own actions, but something involuntary which was happening to Helene, and which she had no power to avert. Erica became more and more concerned that Suzanne had not attempted to visit her mother before taking up her nursing, and in her heart believed that Helene was grieving over it. Not only had she lost her husband, she had lost Wim, and now, just when she needed support so badly, her own daughter appeared to have deserted her.

After about six weeks, Erica noticed in Helene a certain vagueness of manner which accelerated rather than diminished. Erica, eventually realising that she was completely outside Helene's awareness, guessed that it was time to depart. There was really nothing more she could do. She could only hope that rest and time would restore her.

Erica then felt so strongly about the

whole affair that she wanted to admonish Suzanne. After all, Helene *was* her mother, and it was heartless of her not to even visit her, even for a day or two. Erica drew a deep breath. She told herself severely that it was none of her business. But the resentment against Suzanne persisted. She was tempted to pay Suzanne a visit at the hospital, but decided against it. Instead, she would write to her and tell her of her mother's indisposition.

The taxi stopped. She had arrived at her destination. She paid her fare and left the taxi, then went to keep her appointment.

Ten days had passed since Erica had left Helene, but Helene was only half aware that Erica was no longer with her. She stood at the open window of one of the upper rooms of the château which for generations had housed the family of Pascale.

It had been built in the seventeenth century on a hill above the small town which had grown to be at the heart of the French perfume industry.

Far down below she could see the tumbling stone houses which clustered together on the lower slopes, and far away. in the distance, the sea, blue and shining.

She turned her head and raised her eyes to the Esterel mountains where the early morning sun alighted on a bright mantle of mimosa and waves of green. For an instant, memories of her childhood returned to her and she recalled how well acquainted she had been with each and every location. Places where the flowers grew sparsely on the arid soil, and others where the grass was lush and green. Where the herbs caught by the sun between the hot red rocks filled the air with aromatic oils. And above the green and gold of the mimosa, she knew the scent of the pines and the eucalyptus, the myrtle and the juniper.

Through the wide-open window wafted the scent of roses and the wistaria that trailed negligently over a lower balcony, and yellow jasmine in the garden below that. And the pungent clove of carnations, the heavy scent of tuberoses and orange blossom . . . all those magic elements which are the perfumes of Provence in early June.

Yet all these things failed to gladden

Helene's heart as they once had. Her eyes clouded as she remembered Balandra . . . and Wim . . . and finally Edmund. Her heart was heavy and a ceaseless remorse still dragged at her. She had never expected such a reaction at leaving Balandra. And all those years on the island when she had dreamed of home. Well, she was here. But was it home? Was it where she wanted to be? Was anywhere?

She turned to cast her disenchanted eyes around her apartment. The furnishings were just as they always had been, and there had been no need to change the position of even one chair. Her mahogany desk was once more against the wall where it had stood twenty-two years before. On the journey from Martinique one side of it had been smashed. It had been repaired on arrival in France but would never be quite the same again. To Helene, with her passion for perfection, it was a catastrophe, and now, even worse, it was a constant reminder of the wasted years she had spent on Balandra. A shaft of pain caught her breast as she turned away from it and regarded the letter in her hands. Now she opened it. It was from Suzanne.

"Dear Mother," it began. "I am on duty in ten minutes but just had to dash off a few lines to you because Erica wrote yesterday and she says that you aren't well. What's wrong? I do hope you will be feeling better by the time this reaches you.

"I also had a letter from Wim yesterday. He wants to know why you haven't replied to his letters. I've written back to him but didn't know what to say. He says he hasn't heard from you at all. What shall I tell him? . . ."

Helene crumpled the letter in her hands and walked to a chair. She sat down, covering her face with her hands and rocked backwards and forwards. A raging torment took hold of her and she trembled from head to toe. How she longed for Wim . . . longed for the comfort of his arms. She had always been able to count on that. But now Edmund would always come between them. Never would she be able to forgive herself for what she had done. Why, oh why, had this frightful guilt descended upon her? Wim had warned her, years ago: had told her how wrong it was for her to deceive Edmund. She now realised, all too late, that it was not

Edmund's feelings he had been so concerned about, but her own. She had brought it upon herself.

All those years ago he had said to her, "You cannot just brush morality on one side, Helene. Your nature is such that it abhors subterfuge. Edmund would never hold you to your marriage if he knew you wanted your freedom. It is you who hold Edmund—just as surely as if he were on a chain. Why can't you set the poor man free? It isn't even as if he wants to desert you for another woman. All he asks out of life is his work at the hospital. And, dammit, Helene, how to God do you think it makes *me* feel?"

She smoothed open the crumpled pages again, scanned them cursorily then put the letter down on the small table by the window where the breeze caught it and the pages fluttered to the carpet.

Helene got to her feet and went across to a wardrobe. She took out a wide-brimmed hat. I must walk, she told herself. Get away from myself.

The château grounds covered several acres and Helene followed the pathway beneath the old and twisted olive trees.

Beside the path fragrant pinks and lavender grew. She was assailed on all sides by such penetrating beauty that it hurt her all the more.

She walked unheeding for over a mile, making her way slowly she knew not where.

Presently she found herself by the fountain on the Rue de Cours. She stood for a while gazing out across the sunlit bay with its dozens of sailing-craft, the deep blue sea and the curve of clean, shining beach. "It's a different blue from the Caribbean," she mused, then turned and made her way through the crooked streets with their arched stone passages and hidden stairways.

She had no conscious objective, yet found herself at the portals of the Notre-Dame, built and consecrated in the twelfth century.

Helene entered the building and hesitated before the early Fragonard depicting "Christ washing the feet of His Disciples", then moved across the nave to light a candle. She had no money with her to pay for it but was unaware of anything but her desire to kneel, even though her spirit was apathetic. She had not been inside a religious building since her marriage.

She looked up at the Holy Virgin, but no help came. It was as if she had been excommunicated because of her desertion.

Another wave of despair swept over her. "Perhaps Maman was right to try and stop me from marrying Edmund," she thought, remembering how wilfully she had persisted on her own course. "I do not think Maman has ever forgiven me, yet she offers no reproach. I feel so abandoned . . . so alone . . . even Suzanne, my own daughter, has deserted me. I am so weary of life."

Wim's words came back to her once more . . . "Love has to be earned, Helene. Surely you know that." She thought of Wim with tenderness. Never once had he forsaken her, in all those years. In his own special way he had comforted her for her own shortcomings and done all he could to make her happy. He had helped with Suzanne in her most formative years and had been a good influence on her. And yet what would Suzanne become now? Already there was bitterness in her heart. And from whom? Certainly not Wim. He could rise above any difficulties with equanamity and remain the same steadfast man she had always known him to be.

She sought the refuge of a vacant pew, and for an hour or so she sat there in the deserted building, alone with her unhappiness.

The cathedral was cool and quiet, and presently, when she felt calmer, she rose and walked slowly up the central aisle to the door. The sun, even brighter now, freckled through the brim of her straw hat and worried her eyes as she made her way in the direction of the market-place.

Idly she watched the women doing their marketing, imagining their lives to be uncomplicated. She felt weak and confused but made a supreme effort to dismiss it from her mind as she edged closer to the stalls heaped high with the lavish produce of Provence.

The first display she came to was of pies and galantines, decorated beyond belief. Roses of smoked salmon with watercress leaves, carnations fashioned with snipped and tasselled lean pink ham with cooked leek foliage, swans on an aspic lake. Their bodies half a hard-boiled egg, the neck a curled prawn and the head of sculptured butter. Arum lilies wrought from pure white ham fat, a pencil of egg yolk and leaves from carefully cooked pea shells.

All these things Helene had once learned and loved to do. Nostalgia moved her on to the next stall where green and black olives were heaped in profusion, their shiny surfaces fresh as the morning. Dates, aubergines, peppers, figs, peaches, oranges and lemons, haphazard and alluring. Then on to the salads . . . cheeses in profusion, truffles . . . it was all still there, just as she remembered.

She sighed and turned away. Whom could she entertain now? Even that pleasure was ended.

She retraced her steps to the château and, climbing the long, curving staircase, sought the refuge of her own rooms. She threw down her hat and went across to close the shutters against the sun, lay down on her bed and stared at the ceiling. She had not slept for four nights. Perhaps sleep would come to her now.

As she lay there in the darkened room she found herself calling Wim's name, but there was only the buzz of a captive bee to answer. It had come in through a shutter. After a while the bee, also, was silent. No doubt it had found its way to freedom again. If only she could have done the same.

Wim was edgy. For once his plantation irked him.

When the day was done he moved restlessly from one room to another or made pointless small journeys about the neighbourhood, vainly awaiting a letter from Helene. It had been four months now since Edmund had died and he had expected, at least, that she would write to him.

An insidious sense of desertion was creeping up on him and he was experiencing a vulnerability foreign to his nature.

Suzanne, also, had disappointed him. She hadn't written for two months. All he had really received from her was a "heigh-ho I have arrived" note, which told him nothing. He had made repeated pleas for news of her mother. He was distressed. A door had been slammed in his face, and for what reason?

The only letters he could rely on were from Erica. These he valued. There was nothing in her letters to upset him. But she said very little about Helene except a comment in reply to a question he had asked, about whether Suzanne had yet been to see her mother.

His anger mounted. He would go to London and have it out with Suzanne. Then he would go across to France and see Helene, if only to reassure himself that she had adjusted to her new situation. He *must* see her, just *once* more.

He flew to England three days later and at Ogbourne Street Hospital enquired for Nurse Suzanne Grayson.

The Receptionist was impersonal. "Whom shall I say it is?"

"Wim van Branden."

She smiled distantly and rang through to another part of the hospital.

Wim strolled across and sat on a convenient bench across the hallway.

Within a few minutes he saw Suzanne swinging down the passageway. When she saw Wim she slowed down. She could not speak.

He held out his hands to her and she came to him, blinking back tears.

Neither said anything at first, but finally Wim spoke.

"Suzy, you *must* go over and see your mother. You cannot let it go on."

"How do you know I haven't been already?" She raised her unhappy eyes to his.

"Erica wrote to me. She is so worried about her."

Suzanne looked down at the ground.

"Why haven't you been over to see her, Suzy?"

"You know why."

"But she's your mother. Surely she deserves more consideration than you have shown."

"I just can't bring myself to go. I've tried, but I just can't. It's so awful." She took the handkerchief he held out to her and buried her face in it.

"Now *listen* to me, Suzy. This dreadful feeling you have is because you love her so much, and because she has hurt you it is doubly painful for you. You *must* go over and see her. I know you wouldn't want to wound her any more than she is already."

"And what about *my* feelings? Don't I *ever* get any consideration? It's always Mother, Mother, Mother with you. You don't seem bothered about how you've both made *me* feel. I'll *never* get over it. *Never.*"

Wim ignored her outburst. "Well, I can tell you this," he continued, sternly. "If you *don't* go over and see her soon you'll live to regret it for the rest of your life. It will eventually be something you'll *have* to live with . . . and you won't like it . . . not one bit." His voice reached out to her at last.

She moved a step away from him, keeping the handkerchief to her face, but she said, "I can't go this week, anyway. We're short-staffed." There was compliance in her voice.

"Then you'll go as soon as you possibly can?"

She nodded slowly, "I suppose so."

"You promise?"

"Yes, Wim. I promise." She blew her nose and indicated the handkerchief. "May I keep it?"

He smiled. The tension in him was

lessening. He said, "I must go now, but when do you come off duty?"

"At eight o'clock."

"Then I'll be back here at eight and take you out for a meal." He smiled reassuringly.

Suzanne nodded. "I must go, too. I'll see you later, then."

The brittleness had gone. He watched her retrace her steps down the corridor until she got to the corner. She turned to wave and disappeared.

Wim arrived at Nice airport in the early morning.

He had taken the precaution of sending a wire, and Pierre was there to greet him.

The journey from the airport was about twenty miles, and as they travelled Pierre explained Helene's strange, withdrawn manner.

"The trouble is, you understand. . . she will not eat. She has grown so thin we hardly recognise her."

"Does she know that I am coming?"

"Yes."

"What was her reaction?"

"There was no reaction at all. She just

withdrew into herself, as she does so often, now."

Wim was alarmed.

Helene was waiting for them in the downstairs drawing-room.

She rose to her feet and walked unsteadily towards Wim and grasped his hands with desperate fingers. Silent tears came into her dark, troubled eyes and spilled down her thin cheeks.

Wim's heart lurched with pity and love. This was the woman he had loved for as long as he could remember. It had come to this terrible moment.

He took her in his arms, but she felt like a poor ravaged butterfly she was so slight. He felt an ache in his chest at the sadness that enveloped them both.

She said, plaintively, "Is Edmund back from the hospital yet?" Somehow her mind was repeating a well-remembered pattern.

Wim held her closer, tenderly. He was afraid of crushing the poor thin body.

She hid her face in his jacket and whispered, "Tell him I'm sorry. So, so sorry. I couldn't go with him. Wim wouldn't let me." She paused. "Where is he?" She looked up at Wim with a strange expression and unseeing eyes.

"Hush, my love," he whispered, "I am here." His voice was very low and it was difficult for him to speak. He was distraught to realise how ill she was.

"Don't leave me." She plucked at his jacket. "Oh, *please* don't leave me . . . I need you so." Her look was wan and imploring. "My head hurts."

Wim held her gently.

Suddenly she collapsed as she leaned against him. Wim swept her up in his arms and carried her up the wide, curving staircase, Pierre preceding him as he indicated the way.

When they got to the north wing he laid her gently on her bed and took off her shoes. She felt cold to his touch and he wrapped the blankets around her.

She held out her arms to him and he knelt beside the bed to clasp her hands in his. Her eyes were even darker now and held a lost look. "I can't see you," she whispered, "Where are you?"

"I am here, my darling," Wim answered. He knew that she was confused.

Perhaps it was Edmund she sought. . . there was no way of knowing. So he held her hands in his and she kissed them through her silent tears. Then with a heart-rending sob her dark lashes at last came down and she appeared to have fallen into a deep sleep.

Wim stayed where he was for a time, looking down at her with deep compassion until he sensed that something was very wrong.

Pierre was waiting outside. Wim put a hand on his shoulder and said, in a low voice, "I think we had better call the doctor."

The doctor had come immediately. He was very concerned about Helene's condition and said he would make arrangements for her to come into his private clinic the following morning.

"She must have someone with her tonight," he said. "Shall I send up one of my nurses?"

Wim raised a hand. "That won't be necessary, Doctor. I shall be here."

The doctor took a second look at Helene and opened his bag. "I'll give her a sedative tonight," he said. "It will give her a comfortable night." He turned to Wim. "She has been under something of a strain recently, I believe. Losing her husband so soon after their return to France has been a serious shock for her."

Wim nodded. There was no point in telling the full story.

As the doctor left the room, he said, "Keep her warm. She should sleep now."

There was a muffled knock on the half-open door.

Wim went across to admit Madame Pascale. Pierre was beside her. She was very frail and it had been an effort for her to climb the stairs, even with her son's help.

She gave Wim a long, searching look and put her hand on his arm. "So, *you're* the one," she said, barely audibly. Inclining her head she continued, "My daughter should never have left France, but . . ." She made an eloquent movement, "thank you for being good to her." She moved towards the bed with difficulty, placing her hand on the pillow near to Helene's face. For a moment she wavered, then lightly touching the sleeping figure, she bent down and kissed her daughter. Then she straightened up and gazed unflinchingly at Wim. There were no tears. Then she turned to seek Pierre's steadying arm for her return down the long, curved staircase.

Wim maintained his vigil at Helene's bedside. He kept awake through the night, but towards morning he dozed off. He awoke at seven and got up out of the armchair, rebuking himself for having fallen asleep. "How is she," he wondered, treading softly across the carpet to her bed.

Wim looked down upon the beautiful face he had known so well. It was now in complete repose. The dark lashes rested upon the pale cheeks, and as he gazed at her he gradually became aware of the stillness that had passed beyond sleep.

Her hands lay clasped upon the coverlet and he stretched out a hand to cover them with his. Her flesh was cold to his touch.

With an expression of sorrow he bent down and kissed the now serene brow and stood looking down at her for the last time. Then he called Pierre. The doctor would have to be summoned immediately.

When formalities were over and Wim had done his best to cope with his grief at her passing, he said to Pierre, "May I use your telephone? Long distance?"

Pierre nodded. "Of course." His own feelings were numb. He turned to lead Wim to the telephone, then went into the drawing-room to comfort his mother.

Wim got through to the matron of the Ogbourne Street Hospital and requested that the news be broken to Suzanne as gently as possible.

"Do you wish Suzanne to travel over for the funeral?" Matron enquired.

Wim thought quickly. "No," he said, "I think that would distress her too much. Just tell her that I will come to her as soon as I can, after the funeral . . . and Matron, . . . thank you."

He then telephoned a cablegram to Erica. It read:

HELENE DIED PEACEFULLY STOP HAVE INFORMED SUZANNE STOP WILL ARRIVE SOONEST

When the funeral was over and Wim bade farewell to Pierre and Madame Pascale his grief was profound. But in his heart he knew that he had always done his best for Helene, and now nothing could bring her back to him. A long chapter of his life was over and he had to go on living without her.

But first he wanted to see Erica.

If Wim had asked himself why he wanted to see Erica he would have been uncertain of his motive. He only knew that in some mysterious way that Erica had become an important link in their lives. She was someone kind and generous to turn to.

When he arrived at Heathrow he took a taxi, and when it finally drew up to the mews house, the door opened and Erica was waiting.

She held up her hand and called out. "Wait! Hold the taxi." Then grabbing her coat from somewhere behind the door, ran to the taxi and got in beside him.

Wim looked at her. "Where are we going?"

"To Suzanne, of course." Her smile was a caress on his battered spirit.

"She knows we are coming?"

"Yes."

"Is she very distressed?"

"Not so much as she was when Edmund died."

Wim noted that she had not used the word "father". Perhaps she knew. Had Helene told her? Somehow it no longer mattered.

"How about Paul? Does she see him?"

"For a while she did . . . but . . ."

"But what?"

Erica shook her head. "I don't know."

Wim was quiet for a while. Then he said, "Will she settle in England, do you think?"

"There's no knowing. She hasn't said."

Wim's expression saddened. "My only regret is that she didn't go over and see her mother."

Erica didn't reply. There was little she could trust herself to say about Suzanne's behaviour.

Suddenly he turned to her. "I have to get back to my plantation. Erica . . . I want to ask you . . . will you come back with me?" His words came with a rush, unheeded and uncharacteristic.

"You mean . . . to Balandra?"

"Yes."

"What about Suzanne?"

Wim didn't hesitate. "She's on her own, now. I've done all I can for her." Then, as if brushing the subject aside, he turned to Erica and reached out his hand to touch her. "I want you, Erica. I need you. . . so much. Will you marry me?"

Erica placed her hand in his. There was no need for her to speak. Her shining eyes told Wim all he wanted to know.

"You can stay with Claire and Vincent, if you like," he said, "until I have a room ready for you."

Erica knew what he was trying to say.

"Please don't change anything, Wim. Not yet, anyway. Let's take things as they come. I'll stay with Claire, at first, if you want me to . . . but whatever you decide, I'll be very happy to come with you."

In response, Wim sought her hand and brought it gently to his lips. Her touch had a healing quality he had never thought possible.

16

SUZANNE appeared to accept her mother's death with resignation, but Wim knew that she was as yet unable to realise what had happened.

If she had seen her mother, as he himself had seen her, thin and ill and grieving for her lost identity, she would surely have felt very differently. He was concerned for her, but there was little he could do. She would have to resolve her own difficulties from now on.

He and Erica had spent the evening with her, telling her only as much as she needed to know.

Concerning their own relationship, Suzanne had guessed as soon as she saw them together. Erica's manner, betrayed her. She was glowing, despite the sadness of the occasion. When Erica said, quietly, as she and Wim were about to leave, "I'm going back to Balandra with him," Suzanne kissed her impulsively, not quite knowing what remark to make.

"Why am I not jealous?" she asked herself aloud, when they had gone, thinking, "I've loved Wim for so long I thought it would hurt."

Gradually an idea formed in her mind and she went across to consider her reflection in the mirror.

It took only a moment or two to arrive at the inevitable conclusion. The same blonde hair, the same deep blue eyes as his looked back at her. Ever since those few moments alone with him at the airport she had pondered his words about her childhood, and the idea had taken shape from that time.

"So *that's* why I've always felt so close to him!" She looked even more searchingly at her image, tracing the line of her jaw with her hand and speculating. Emotion overcame her as she clasped her hands and whispered, "I'm glad he's my father. So glad."

She no longer felt lost. New heart had come into her, and it was at that moment she resolved that whatever she did in the future she would follow Wim's example and follow through any task she began.

She still felt no penitence for not going

to France, however. She told herself that her mother had never shown her much affection. It had only been Wim who ever considered her at all.

Now he had Erica. She loved them both. Ever since she had first set eyes on Erica she, too, had loved her. How could anyone *help* loving Erica?

She smiled to herself as she thought of Ben's last letter and his suggestion. She hadn't told them. It would be a surprise. Perhaps she would tell them in a month or two, after they were married.

Suzanne went on with her training for the statutory three years, and when she had passed her exams and qualified for her SRN she left Ogbourne Street Hospital and England for good.

Once again she was seated in the small aircraft that ferried passengers between Trinidad and Balandra, and once again she looked out along the silver wing to the green islands below, the shining sands forever running out to sea beneath the crystal clear water.

As the pilot few lower and closer to Balandra she searched in vain for the blue lake, but she couldn't see it. It must have been on the other side of the mountains.

The coffee plantation looked at its best. Wim and Erica were married now and soon she would visit them.

As they came into land a joyous feeling rose within her and her heart raced. Would Ben be there?

Soon she saw the red Pinto skim the airfield perimeter and come to rest as near to the landing-strip as was permitted. Then she spotted a second vehicle. It was Wim's station wagon! And then a third, following his. A familiar Range Rover.

Excitement churned. Coming home before had never been like this.

She looked down at her wrist and fingered the gold chain bracelet which she had grown to love wearing, and once again her heart was light and she was full of optimism for the future.

She unfastened her safety belt and stood up, letting the folds of her cream silk dress adjust themselves, then found her way to the exit.

At the top of the steps she lingered, wondering if she had forgotten anything.

But of course not. She had bequeathed her fox coat to Jill.

She looked towards the visitors' enclosure. They were all waving to her. She smiled tremulously, her eyes misting so that she could hardly see.

Wim and Erica, Claire and Vinny, and Ben, especially Ben. He had become the most dear of all to her.

After Customs had inspected her baggage she walked through the building to where they were all waiting.

At first she only had eyes for Ben.

He came steadily towards her, slightly solemn as ever, and she ran to him eagerly. And now they were in each other's arms and Ben was kissing her. She would be sharing the remainder of her life with him.

Happiness had come to Suzanne at last.

GUIDE
TO THE COLOUR CODING
OF
ULVERSCROFT BOOKS

Many of our readers have written to us expressing their appreciation for the way in which our colour coding has assisted them in selecting the Ulverscroft books of their choice. To remind everyone of our colour coding— this is as follows:

BLACK COVERS
Mysteries

★

BLUE COVERS
Romances

★

RED COVERS
Adventure Suspense and General Fiction

★

ORANGE COVERS
Westerns

★

GREEN COVERS
Non-Fiction

ROMANCE TITLES
in the
Ulverscroft Large Print Series

The Smile of the Stranger	*Joan Aiken*
Busman's Holiday	*Lucilla Andrews*
Flowers From the Doctor	*Lucilla Andrews*
Nurse Errant	*Lucilla Andrews*
Silent Song	*Lucilla Andrews*
Merlin's Keep	*Madeleine Brent*
Tregaron's Daughter	*Madeleine Brent*
The Bend in the River	*Iris Bromige*
A Haunted Landscape	*Iris Bromige*
Laurian Vale	*Iris Bromige*
A Magic Place	*Iris Bromige*
The Quiet Hills	*Iris Bromige*
Rosevean	*Iris Bromige*
The Young Romantic	*Iris Bromige*
Lament for a Lost Lover	*Philippa Carr*
The Lion Triumphant	*Philippa Carr*
The Miracle at St. Bruno's	*Philippa Carr*
The Witch From the Sea	*Philippa Carr*
Isle of Pomegranates	*Iris Danbury*
For I Have Lived Today	*Alice Dwyer-Joyce*
The Gingerbread House	*Alice Dwyer-Joyce*
The Strolling Players	*Alice Dwyer-Joyce*
Afternoon for Lizards	*Dorothy Eden*
The Marriage Chest	*Dorothy Eden*

THE SHADOWS
OF THE CROWN TITLES
in the
Ulverscroft Large Print Series

FICTION TITLES
in the
Ulverscroft Large Print Series

The Onedin Line: The High Seas
Cyril Abraham
The Onedin Line: The Iron Ships
Cyril Abraham
The Onedin Line: The Shipmaster
Cyril Abraham
The Onedin Line: The Trade Winds
Cyril Abraham
The Enemy   *Desmond Bagley*
Flyaway   *Desmond Bagley*
The Master Idol   *Anthony Burton*
The Navigators   *Anthony Burton*
A Place to Stand   *Anthony Burton*
The Doomsday Carrier *Victor Canning*
The Cinder Path *Catherine Cookson*
The Girl   *Catherine Cookson*
The Invisible Cord *Catherine Cookson*
Life and Mary Ann *Catherine Cookson*
Maggie Rowan   *Catherine Cookson*
Marriage and Mary Ann *Catherine Cookson*
Mary Ann's Angels *Catherine Cookson*
All Over the Town *R. F. Delderfield*
Jamaica Inn   *Daphne du Maurier*
My Cousin Rachel *Daphne du Maurier*

NON-FICTION TITLES
in the
Ulverscroft Large Print Series

MYSTERY TITLES
in the
Ulverscroft Large Print Series